Circumcised
at Seventeen

A Previously Uncut Comedy

Circumcised at Seventeen

at Seventeen

A Previously Uncut Comedy

Brian Robert Smith

3 **23**ooks

Toronto, Canada

Canadian Intellectual Property Office Registration Number: 1122769

Library of Congress Registration Number: PAu003485034

ISBN (paperback first edition): 978-1-988063-01-0

Published by 323 Books, Ontario, Canada

Cover Design by artistraman.com

Printed in the U. S. A.

DEDICATION

To Sacha, Jazz, and Shyanne.

Their youth inspires me; their love motivates me, and their honesty makes me try harder.

CHAPTER 1

He would have preferred being in a quiet place, just him and his lunch; but, *not this time,* as his best friend, Will, had insisted. During this particular noon hour, Hubert Rawlings sat within the sea of tables at a shopping center food court.

Hubert was fine with being at the shopping center to satisfy Will's sense of adventure, but having to eat here was nerve wracking to Hubert. It shouldn't have been a big deal. This place was just like all other food courts, and he should be able to escape into his own world here like anywhere else. There was a difference, though.

Although the vast table area surrounded a wide range of fast food options, there were few choices when it came to companions for Hubert. Population was not the issue: his popularity was.

He'd always considered this place some sort of

1

informal teenaged social headquarters, and he never saw himself fitting in. Will seemed determined to change that. They were missing out on their teenage experience which frustrated Will to his boiling point. So this was where lunch would be today, Hubert thought while sitting awkwardly as though he had a fifty foot restraining order against all others around.

With his head down, a food tray carrying a plate of cheese fries and gravy startled Hubert. It crashed into his garden salad. He was determined to appear undisturbed and focused. He picked his salad for precise selection; although, his nerves rattled from the disturbance.

He watched a fork begin to assault the fries.

"As soon as they get to my app..."

It was Will talking and now sitting with him, but Hubert had no intention to reveal his nervousness. Looking up would do just that, so he watched the fork. It took a break. Hubert continued dissecting his salad.

"I tell ya, man, workin' here—it'll be like no other place," Will said.

Hubert knew what Will was going on about. They had both applied for work here a few weeks back, again at Will's insistence. Since then, Will seemed convinced he was in, and working with the shopping center's maintenance crew would be his one way ticket to teenage success. Hubert understood Will's plan, but the social nightmare that would result was a scary thought to say the least.

Hubert looked away and saw a table wiper cleaning next to them. He was young, hot as hell, and Hubert noticed every girl nearby watching him work. This was the exact problem Hubert had with being here in the first place. He couldn't compete with that, even if Will thought otherwise.

The fork loaded up with more fries. Hubert had his fork almost full with lettuce. He chomped down on it to continue his disguised distraction.

"Two weeks tops, I'm in. From then on..."

From the corner of Hubert's eye, he saw another worker grabbing a tray from another table.

"I'll be pickin' panties off all those hottie bushes," Will concluded.

The worker stacked the tray in a pile that he could easily start juggling any minute. The two workers worked magic with trays and cloths: sidewalk entertainment in the food court, and much too close to them in Hubert's frazzled opinion.

Hubert winced as another worker broke in with a pail and a wet mop. In came a garbage worker slinging garbage bags with both hands. He was catching throws from all callers.

Hubert watched the table wiper break away for a throw. The garbage worker stepped back with an empty ice tea bottle.

The table wiper weaved in and out of tables.

The garbage worker set up for a clear throw. He launched the bottle.

It was up, heading straight for the table; straight at Hubert.

Even though he was trying desperately to go unnoticed, he was in the line of fire and had to move. He turned and exposed his innocent face: pure, sweet, and cuddly. Shit, it was a wonder this kid still had all his teeth.

Hubert saw the table wiper behind the airborne bottle. The table wiper surged for another table then launched off it with one foot.

Hubert ducked. He covered up looking like a freaked out Boy Scout with a mouthful of lettuce.

The table wiper made the catch right before a direct hit. He landed as if nothing happened.

Will jumped up seeming eager to make a lasting impression. Hubert knew Will would be unsuccessful, though. He was really just a teenaged tubby who saw himself as buff, but he was the only one.

Fries flew. Hubert watched a sample of something land in the mess.

Will pulled an invisible flag from his hip pocket. "Table interference. Defense! Declined!"

Hubert watched Will waiting for a reaction: nothing.

Will sat back down. His hand slipped in the mess. He seemed suddenly flustered—embarrassed. "Shit, Pubes, who's gonna hire me when they see I hang with a primate?" He looked around for others watching. Luckily, this time at least, no one cared, Hubert thought.

Hubert rushed to clean up. "Shouldn't you be trying to attract a different audience?"

Will picked out the sample with gravy dripping from it. He wiped it off. "Pubes, man, really. Learn to dance with others who dance."

Hubert watched Will fiddling with the sample. It could have easily been tossed aside as garbage, but Hubert knew Will had no intention of passing on this gem. "It's probably better to stick with an existing skill set, don't ya think?"

Will looked up, offended. He paused with the sample, apparently realizing his grip on it was too tight. "No, Pubes, I don't!" He pocketed the sample. "Getting a skill from workin' here is what I'm set on."

Hubert looked reluctantly to the crew of workers who were taking in all the female attention they could get. He nodded, slowly. He turned his attention back to the salad, discouraged.

Hubert had news for Will. How Will would take it, Hubert had no idea; but this was probably as good a time as any to find out. "I start Monday," Hubert said, reluctantly.

Will froze. He started to respond but stopped short of any words coming out. He cracked a slight smile.

And, do you have to call me Pubes all the time?

CHAPTER 2

Hubert hugged a wall and stared at another three feet away. It was well lit in this lifeless hallway but ominous just the same. Despite this dingy environment he was already in, a little darker would have been better, he thought. Having some place to hide behind, or around, or beneath would be nice too. Just as his luck would have it, though, he was fully exposed. It was only a matter of time—seconds really—that the obnoxious locker room chatter, coming from a room at the end of the hall, would be focused on him. At this point, there was simply no way around the facts. He was about to meet his crewmates.

As Hubert stood frozen to the wall, he couldn't help but think about how he'd gotten himself into this mess. Really, it had little to do with him. It was all Will's dream to work with these guys, but somehow Hubert was the one who got the starring role. Will had envisioned himself on the shopping center's maintenance crew. He got hold of the applications. He even filled out Hubert's information. Hubert just signed the form and forgot about the whole idea. Now, Will's plan was in full execution, and Hubert was doing the dirty work.

This was often the way Hubert's friendship with Will went. Will would get high on an idea, and Hubert would be forced to go along for the ride. For the most part Hubert didn't mind. Most of the stuff Will had come up with made life interesting, and none of it ever transpired into anything Hubert hadn't been able to deal with.

When they were kids, Will's plans usually had something to do with staying busy in the summertime. Since nothing was thought out well on Will's part, Hubert's involvement could make or break the deal. That advantage had always given Hubert some kind of control, and he could usually make things fall perfectly in line with his lack of social skills. This was a conclusion he much preferred over Will's dream of adolescent acceptance.

Will had stepped it up when they got to high school, however. His focus was on one thing and one thing only: their popularity.

During the very first week, Will saw the Student Council as his claim to fame. His only problem with living the life of a council member would be the decisions he'd be force to make, so he had set Hubert up to run for President. It was a great idea having both of them on council, but that idea died quickly after the bulletin board posters he made for both of them became canvases for the school's creative pranksters.

Another time, during spring break, he forced Hubert to be first in the door when they showed up uninvited at a massive house party. "*Just make like you own the place*," Will kept saying. But after Hubert had made it in without anyone caring at all, he noticed Will hadn't followed him. Being in there all alone made Hubert way too nervous, so he backtracked his steps and left out the door he had come in.

Outside, Will was sitting on the curb by himself. He was embarrassed because he didn't have the nerve Hubert just had. The reality of it was that Hubert didn't have any nerve either. He was just moving like a robot really, with Will handling the remote.

After that Will was determined to find a way to fit in, so they started spending time at the food court just like everyone else. From doing that, and basically only staring at each other, Will had come up with the maintenance crew idea.

This plan was different, though. It was a job—a first job—and the possibility of it actually happening was real. Hubert had never taken it seriously because of all the failures from the past. It wasn't until Hubert got a call from the crew's supervisor—*Shit, what was his name again?* That call led to an interview which Hubert thought he would have no chance getting through. But the talk with Rod—*yes, Rod is his name*—had gone well because Rod didn't appear to care about who his next hire would be. He seemed satisfied with having a face in front of him and anxious to get this hiring process out of the way. So, after a few sentences of small talk, Hubert was given a start date and time. Both of which were right now.

Hubert took a quick look at his watch. Actually, he wasn't supposed to start now. He was late…

He took a deep breath and pushed himself from the wall. Just like his experience at the house party, Hubert didn't have the balls for this. At this point, however, he didn't see himself having much choice. Slowly, he moved forward, one foot in front of the other. A closed door was his destination. Unfortunately, he would get there too soon.

The door he faced now represented his last chance to bail, but it was also the only barrier between himself and the rest of the world. At least that's the way Will would see it, and Hubert felt like he should look at this opportunity the same way. Just a push on the door could change everything for him. Just a push… The door wasn't even shut. He could hear them inside the room. He should want this just like Will did. He understood how important it was to take the next step, but if he did that, there would be no turning back this time.

Just push on the door…

At first, no one noticed Hubert standing there. He had pushed the door open, but he didn't step inside the room. He saw a guy taking a piss in an open view urinal. Two other guys were topless, sitting at a lunch table. Certainly, there was nothing private here, and the fact that Hubert stood at the door was no different. But no one seemed to care...

That was instantly relieving for Hubert, but just as he began to relax, a locker door creaked. Suddenly, Hubert was the feature.

The guy peeing turned. The guys at the table turned.

The locker door slammed shut with a teenaged beast standing in front of it. He headed straight for Hubert.

Hubert didn't move. He couldn't move. It was as though he was frozen by testosterone.

The guy kept coming, framed with his crew who had slipped in behind him as if they had planned Hubert's introduction all along. The guy was straight faced and intimidating as hell, like Arnold as the Terminator.

Hubert was ready to melt, but the guy grew a smile. It was too big to take seriously, though. He forced a fist bump and turned Hubert around almost in the same motion.

"New guy, Homies," the guy said. He waited for a response from Hubert. The guy rolled his finger. "Name..."

"Oh, sorry. Hubert. I'm Hubert Rawlings. Today I start

my Molly Maid apprenticeship."

Hubert had thought about using that line to break the ice, but now he wished he hadn't. He smiled, awkwardly, but not the mountain standing beside him.

"You callin' me a Molly Maid?"

"No, man, sorry. Just trying to—"

"Hubert. Who names their kid Hubert?"

"Well, my friend calls me..." Hubert hesitated. He gritted his teeth. "Pubes."

The guy was confused. "Why?"

"He says, 'Hubert, rhymes with puber...ty. Pubes for short.'"

The guy looked away with wrinkled eyebrows: confused by the logic. He shook his head. "Never mind. I like it."

He suddenly lost interest in Hubert and addressed the others. "Call him Pubes. Short, skinny, all shriveled up. Makes sense to me." He left. He went back to his locker and found interest in a new cell phone, still in the box.

Just like that, introductions were done. When the big guy left, so did everyone else. All that Hubert had stressed about appeared to be over. That wasn't so bad, he thought. Not bad at all... The only problem Hubert had now was...

What's next?

He was still at the door. No one told him where to go or what to do. He watched others, and the lockers seemed to be where everyone was going. He focused on an unused locker and saw his name on it. Now, at least he had his answer, but he had no clue if the trip across the room to that locker would be successful.

An uneventful crossing got him there. He didn't trip or bump into anything. From what Hubert could tell, he was already just one of the guys. It seemed unlikely, but nothing was telling Hubert otherwise.

He noticed all the chiseled guys that lined the row of lockers. Everyone seemed to have a similar focus although no one was in any great hurry. Hubert opened his door and saw his uniform. He looked around cautiously while he started fumbling with his shirt buttons. His next step was to change. *How am I ever going to get through this?*

The big guy was two lockers away and dressed only in boxers. He struggled with the cell phone that he now had out of the box. "Just give me the bare essentials dammit!" He fired a ripping stare directly at Hubert.

Hubert thought, just like at the door, the big guy's lead would get everyone watching him. Changing in front of an audience was something Hubert didn't think he could do. It was something he certainly didn't want to do.

The big guy held up the phone in frustration. "Anyone know how this thing works?"

Another guy plucked it from his grasp.

Hubert tried to cover himself behind his locker door as the other guy zipped by.

"Embrace your possession, Chester. Learn to free yourself from the fear of the unknown," he said then turned quickly and snapped a picture of Chester.

Okay, one problem was solved, Hubert thought. *His name is Chester. Please don't forget that.*

Chester was amazed. "How'd you do that, Tony?" Chester chased after him.

The phone flew across the room. Another guy picked it out of the air.

Chester stopped with no intention of playing fetch-the-phone. Hubert struggled to get his shirt off when he saw Chester heading back toward him.

"Come on, show me the goods. There's no need for these hideaway games."

Hubert covered up a little. He was confused about who Chester was talking to.

The guy with the phone snapped a shot of everyone along the locker row, including Hubert.

Others perked up for some posing shots. One was topless and full flexed. Another stripped down for a Playboy pose.

Chester was fuming. "Cut it with the gay pics, Drew." He surged for the phone. Another guy stepped in his way. He was knocked over a bit which forced Chester to ram him in the butt.

Another shot flashed. The room broke into hysterics. Even Hubert broke up.

Chester chuckled. He shook his head. He looked at Hubert and then gave him a King Kong pose. "Careful, Pubes. Wishes come true."

Drew stopped stone cold. "That's weird. What would you call it, Tony?"

"Ummm, use of extreme masculinity to intimidate the new guy, in a strange kinda way."

"But it's not funny," Drew said.

"That's right. You're not funny, Chester."

Among all the chaos, Hubert saw his new boss, Rod, step into the room. Hubert knew him as the maintenance crew supervisor, but now he just looked like one of the guys.

"Two minutes," Rod said.

Hubert saw the look on Rod's face. He didn't seem sure about what to do. He shook his head, looking at a room full of what he wished he hadn't seen. He turned to leave.

"Uniforms on. Two minutes." He continued shaking his head and started talking to himself, but loud enough so Hubert could hear. "Why don't we ask about this stuff in the interview?"

"Rod, Rod," Drew called out.

Hubert started rushing because of Rod's instructions. He was determined to hide at the same time.

Chester's frustration with his camera was back. "Who's gonna delete these?" He was trying to do it himself, but he had no clue how. He was just about ready to toss it.

Drew continued, "Rod! Crew shot!"

Chester looked up and straight at Hubert. Hubert's pants were around his ankles now. Chester slammed the phone into Hubert's hand and said nothing. His look said it all. *Delete or die.*

Hubert worked the phone like magic. In seconds he was finished. *Just hand it back and slip away, right into the locker if you have to.*

Drew snapped the phone from Hubert and sent it flying to Rod.

Hubert suddenly realized he was surrounded by everyone else in the room. With a closer look, he saw they were all naked.

Reluctantly, Rod held up the phone.

Hubert was stunned.

Someone yanked down his briefs. The phone flashed...

Rod looked at the phone. He smiled slightly while shaking his head. He thumbed the keyboard quickly then sent it flying back to Chester.

"One minute now," Rod said.

Chester passed the phone to Hubert. "Classic moment I'm sure, but no male porn stays on my stuff."

Hubert looked at the screen: *Facebook.*

He hesitated then moved to the picture folder. One picture showed. It was the crew shot with Hubert front and center.

He deleted it.

CHAPTER 3

Chester approached a table in the food court occupied by a group of extremely hot chicks. He had the confidence of Mr. Clean that came from his extensive experience with a wet cloth and a hungry smile. He nudged his way through making sure the girls had a chance to experience just a brush of his masculinity. Meticulously, almost in slow motion, he wiped the table top.

He had no intention to speed up this cleaning process. He had no reason to either. He always got their attention, and he would be able to keep it for as long as he was there. Just like all the times he'd cleaned tables for hotties before, Chester felt his job was to give them an experience that would keep them coming back for more.

At least Chester thought it was all about him. For some reason, however, things were different this time. The girls moved away barely realizing he existed. He stood up completely confused as he watched them leave. He looked to another table where Drew seemed to be having the same problem.

In fact, as he scanned the whole area, he noticed all the girls in the food court were zoned in on their cell phones.

***

Two of those girls were Elle and Jane who scurried past the food vendors and navigated their way through hungry customers. They were moving as though they were late for something, but really that wasn't the case. Their hastiness was only motivated by leaving the impression that they were way too busy to be hanging around here.

Elle looked away from her phone. She held it out as though it was contaminated. She commented, "God, that's so…" She closed her eyes. "It's like a finger puppet without character."

Jane laughed. She shook her head in disgust, careful to keep her distance from the phone.

***

Will was here too. He was by himself and searching. He moved quickly from the table section and almost knocked into Elle and Jane.

He plowed on as though they didn't exist and stopped

in front of a Chinese food place: *T-Woks*. He took a second to check himself out in the sneeze glass.

Satisfied with what he had to offer, he couldn't help but notice a girl. She was as confident as a fifth-degree black belt, standing patiently behind the counter. Her name tag said: *Leigh*.

In a bad Chinese accent, Leigh said, "Your order, Sir?"

Will turned, looking confused but not really acknowledging Leigh. "Fuckin' creepy..." He looked up and jumped back. "Uhh! You're white. Someone might die for this."

Leigh faked her embarrassment, apparently just now realizing she was the only one behind the counter that was not Chinese. She smiled, huge. "Your order," she continued, again with a bad accent.

"No, no, sorry. The noodle I'm lookin' for ain't for eatin'." Will turned away and kept looking. He shouldn't be ignoring this girl who was actually talking to him, but he was here for a reason and had to stay focused.

He'd tried to get hold of Pubes before coming here but didn't have any luck. He knew Pubes was starting with the maintenance crew today. The chances of Pubes being here were slim since he could be anywhere in the shopping center, but Will's first thought was to try here. If there was anywhere Pubes would need his help, it would be around all these sweet menu options. He postured up for a group of giggling girls who swept right in front of him. After all, it was *Pubes* he was looking for.

Elle and Jane appeared at the counter, right beside Will.

Jane said, "Leigh, have you seen this?" Jane showed Leigh her phone while taking plastic utensils and a wet towelette.

Will couldn't resist ignoring what they were talking about. He watched Leigh take a look. She raised her eyebrows. She started serving from the vegetable tray without taking her eyes off the phone.

Will saw what was on the phone too but only slightly. He tried to get a closer look. He had to see that again. It couldn't possibly be what he thought he saw. He stepped in closer, but Jane moved away as though he might poison her.

Will fumbled desperately through his pocket to find his own phone. He pulled it out and brushed it off quickly. He started pushing buttons and tapping the screen to get it started.

***

Hubert walked slowly with Rod toward the door of the locker room. Hubert was keen to be learning his new responsibilities, but he was with Rod now. Hubert was more relaxed with Rod, but judging by the look of what he'd seen already, these instructions were likely to be few and far between. If Rod told him anything at all, Hubert better get it right the first time, he thought.

When Hubert had first walked in here, the guys appeared to be in no great hurry to get anything done or go anywhere. After Rod had given the two minute warning, they moved like lightning. They suddenly became organized. They screwed around but dressed quickly, *and the picture...* Then, without notice, Hubert had been left there alone with Rod; and once again, Hubert had no clue what to do.

"For now... Hubert... Just keep moving and cleaning." Rod gave Hubert a look over. "You know, a nickname might be appropriate."

"My friend calls me..." Hubert looked away indecisively. "Forget it. Hubert's fine."

"You might find it a bit distracting on the floor. Just remember the mission statement."

Hubert straightened up, confident. "A unique commitment to satisfy with my greatest asset..." Hubert reverted to confusion. "Forgot the asset," he confessed.

"Pride, Hubert. Your greatest asset is pride, of a job well done. Don't worry, though. Chester and Drew will be close by, and I'll be watching out for ya."

***

Hubert opened a door and stood there, reluctant to take the plunge into the depths of the shopping center.

Washrooms were straight ahead, at the other side of the hall. He could easily just duck in there with the excuse that he had to go. That wouldn't do him much good, though, other than delay the inevitable.

Rod had just told him to clean and keep moving. Those were his boss's instructions, but Hubert was still clueless. He couldn't clean because he had nothing to clean with, and he had no idea what he should be cleaning. All he could do now was move, but he preferred to stay here, stuck to the security of a door he could easily hide behind if he needed to.

Probably the best thing for him to do was find Chester. To do that, he would have to step away from the door. He sighed and walked into the hallway.

Having to search through the whole shopping center for someone he didn't really want to find was probably a good way for Hubert to start this job. He would be on his own. He had no idea where to search, so it would probably take a while. In fact, it looked to Hubert that he could take as long as he wanted. No one had told him what to do at this point, so there was absolutely nothing he could be doing wrong.

After a few steps, he stopped. Hubert realized where he was. It wasn't the whole shopping center he would have to search through to find Chester because he could see him already, along with Drew and all the other food court loiterers. It was tables Rod expected him to be cleaning, but this cleaning crew did more to work the area than polish table tops. Surely Rod didn't expect a circus act from him too...

Before Hubert could get his legs moving again, Chester was right in front of him. Hubert didn't know what he'd done wrong, but the look on Chester's face told him he was about to find out. Chester just turned away, though, giving Hubert a chance to see Drew staring him down from a distance.

Hubert definitely did something that pissed these two off, but what? A rolled up, dry towel banged against his chest. *I've done nothing...* He looked directly at Chester knowing the towel came from him. He turned away immediately after seeing Chester's intimidating stare.

A wet towel slapped Hubert in the face. He watched it fall to the floor. *Maybe they want me to stop doing nothing and start working...* He bent over to pick up the towel. He hesitated, almost certain to be bombarded with more rags.

That never happened, and quickly he was alone again. At least now he had something to work with. He looked at his hands holding the tools of a food court cleaner. Hubert snuck up to an empty table. He cleaned it efficiently. The wet cloth in one hand, and the dry one in the other. He moved on to another table: no problem.

After cleaning the second table, he looked up. There was a problem now. The two tables he'd just cleaned were the only empty ones in the whole food court. He had no choice about what to do next, so he quickly braved up and moved into a more populated area.

Some girls started to sit at a messed up table. He rushed to get it ready by moving the trays away and wiping it clean. He motioned for them to take a seat with a welcoming smile. They watched, but they didn't sit down.

One Girl reached quickly for her phone, then the other three did the same.

A hand touched Hubert's while he was picking up the trays. It was soft, gentle. He stopped, but didn't look up.

All he'd done was clean their table... He had given them a nice smile... Hubert was stressed about many things that would likely happen today, but this... He hadn't even considered it. He moved away quickly. He was confused, disoriented, like the room was suddenly a maze. He was not sure where to go with the trays or which way to turn. Girls were everywhere, and they were all watching him.

Suddenly, Will was right there, and he could hardly contain himself. "Brilliant! Fucking brilliant, man!"

"What?"

Hubert didn't get any of what was suddenly happening. He noticed a girl nearby giving him the classic schoolgirl hooker look. Another sat at the table they were beside and opened up for a private upskirt shot.

"I can't believe it, Pubes. You're a fuckin' woman windfall."

"I'm what?"

Hubert tried to distract himself with desperate cleaning. He slid his wet cloth straight into a fat lady's garden salad and knocked over her Diet Coke.

He rushed to the floor to clean up the mess. Will stayed with him. The fat lady looked furiously at Will.

"Who the fuck ya kiddin'. He just did you a favor," Will said directly to her.

Will got on his knees, to Hubert's level. "You've got the utensil to serve hottie helpings. You're carrying a babe basket."

Hubert gave Will a look of extreme confusion. "That doesn't make any sense, Will. None of this makes sense."

Hubert got up and saw Chester converging with the rest of the crew. They were all looking at him.

He needed to stay away from them. He went to get a tray stacked over the garbage. He grabbed one, but the rest crashed to the floor.

A kid carrying his kiddy combo stepped on one. Hubert watched him falling, and more food flew.

Will was still in hot pursuit after Hubert but was blocked by the wreckage. He stopped at the Kid who seemed to expect Will to help him. "Three skimpy chicken nuggets. Man up, kid, with the burger and special order cheese fries."

Hubert moved quickly to a mop and bucket at a cleaning station. *Keep your head down and stay busy...*

Will relentlessly maintained his chase. "You're a friggin' lady lord," he said right into Hubert's ear.

"I'm scared, Will." Scared of what, Hubert had no idea.

He pulled out the wet mop and slapped it right on the cowboy boot of a huge Texan wearing a ten gallon hat. The Texan kicked the mop away.

Hubert followed it and turned back to see Will caught face-to-face with the Texan.

"Big boots. Big feet. Congrats!" Will said with a huge grin.

Hubert grabbed the mop handle. Chester was at the other end. Hubert froze.

Will was there in a flash. He took the mop and pushed it to Chester. "He won't need this. His cleanup is already done."

Hubert quickly turned away and was on the run again with loyal Will chasing. Will caught him and stopped him right in front of T-Woks.

Will turned him around. "It's a good thing, Pubes. It's a great—"

Hubert pulled Will in close. He took a deep breath. "Why me, Will? Why—" None of this made any sense. All he wanted was this attention to vanish.

Will pushed his phone to Hubert's face, and there it was. The crew picture.

"Look close," Will said.

Hubert focused in. He was front and center, looking

totally confused and disorientated. The crew surrounded him. They were all naked; Hubert was naked.

That was enough to totally embarrass him, but it still didn't justify all the attention. Something else was in play here. He could feel the whole area closing in on him. The answer wasn't coming to him, and he didn't feel like sticking around to see how everything played out.

He looked away and directly at a girl behind the counter ready to take his order. He quickly noticed her name tag.

Will nudged him desperately, trying to get Hubert's attention back on the picture. "You're sportin' a hoodie while everyone else wears a helmet," Will said.

Leigh asked Hubert in her bad accent, "Your order, Sir?"

"He'll have two sides of poontang. Extra heat on mine," Will answered.

Will couldn't resist a quick peek in the sneeze glass. He turned to take in all the attention, but suddenly, he held his arms out as if to say, *stop everything!*

Straight ahead, staring straight at Hubert, was Virginia Almond, the Goddess of the Food Court.

Hubert knew about Virginia Almond. Will knew about her. Everyone did...

"Hubert, Pubes, Rawlings..." Will stepped back. "You, my friend..."

Virginia stepped forward.

"Are the wearer of the golden sleeve," Will concluded.

Hubert saw Will bowing, giving Hubert the spotlight. Hubert turned away sharply. He was stopped by the counter and a front line of Chinese chefs behind it.

He had to get out of here, but he couldn't go right, Chester and the crew were there.

Rod was heading his way from the left looking like he was ready to pull the pitcher.

And of course, straight ahead was…

Fuck it! He jumped the counter and landed face-to-face with Leigh. The moment stopped him. Leigh suddenly lost her confidence. Hubert lost himself in her eyes but only briefly.

His surge away from her put him straight into a barrel chest and another name tag: *Tung.* Hubert looked up to the eyes of a Chinese War Lord dressed in a stained, white cooking apron.

Hubert bolted for the kitchen.

CHAPTER 4

Pots crashed behind him as Hubert faced another wall in another narrow hallway. He considered going left, but boxes labelled *Fortune Cookies* were blocking a clear path. A lot of Chinese screaming motivated him the other way. Within two steps, he was through a doorway and into a small storage room.

Hubert kept moving, but he was stopped by a counter and an impatient, female fashionista on the other side. "Six inch, ham only. Absolutely no cheese. On whole wheat with lettuce, tomatoes, pickles and balsamic vinaigrette," she instructed directly at Hubert.

Hubert said nothing. She looked up, silent also, except for her body language which said, *got a problem with that?*

Next to Hubert was a team of Pakistani ladies, staring. He turned to the cash register and saw another name tag: *Abid.* Hubert cautiously looked up, and Abid was peering

31

over his glasses. Abid shifted his cap labelled: *Sub Attack*.

Hubert saw Tung from T-Woks waving his arms frantically. "Abid, Abid, the boy. Stop the boy," he yelled in a good Chinese accent.

Hubert bolted again, back into the hallway.

He rounded the corner from Sub Attack and suddenly stopped, face-to-face with a short Mexican. The Mexican wobbled back and struggled to balance the large stack of hard taco shells he held in each hand.

"Ahhh! No, no, no. No break the taco," the Mexican cried in broken English.

Hubert sidestepped him, careful not to make contact. The Mexican recovered. He smiled.

Hubert caught a peek of the Chinese chefs chasing him with their knives slicing the air. Not sure where to go next, he found refuge behind a stack of hamburger buns.

A tuned out, twenty-something guy grabbed a tray and missed Hubert hiding there completely, although his name tag brushed by Hubert's nose. Hubert couldn't help but notice his name: *Mark*.

Mark turned away to the crash of tacos followed by mixed Chinese and Spanish yelling. Mark cried out among the chaos, "Christ, Javier, not again. My gut's screaming' Mexican Heaven. Now what's going to fill the pit?"

The distraction would give Hubert some time but only if he kept moving. He noticed a closed door beside him. He opened it regardless of what he quickly read on the sign: *Italy's Best - Employees only. Others will pay...* The warning made him think, but didn't slow him down. At this point, Hubert had no other choice.

Inside, the pounding of pizza dough hitting a counter stopped Hubert instantly. The look on the face of an angry Dough Master turned Hubert right around.

While fleeing, Hubert turned to see the Dough Master looking out his door. He confronted Mark in a thick Italian accent, "You need a reminder about your homeboys?"

"Chill, Rocco, chill," Mark replied. Mark stepped back so Rocco could see the Chinese and Mexican disaster. "Enjoy the free show, dude."

Rocco smiled. "Hungry taco lovers always go for pizza slices. Javier doesn't need to be reminded of that," he said and slammed Italy's Best's door shut.

Hubert got some distance, but the Chinese madmen spotted him. They chased relentlessly, yelling like hyper pocket dogs.

Hubert fled around a corner and saw another closed door: *Chicken Fried Right.*

He needed to get behind one of these doors in case the knives started flying. Hubert peered in from the hallway, cautious this time. Black dudes in full-length white aprons worked the fryers. They saw Hubert immediately. Hubert paused then checked the store sign on the door. He looked back.

One guy stepped up: apron, Bluetooth ear piece—the whole package. His name tag identified him as: *Tyrell*. "That's right, black dudes in a fried chicken shop. What's your order?"

Hubert hit the gas again. This time he directly entered a door and closed it quickly as the screaming Chinese crew flew by.

In here, four short, fat ladies wearing flowery, *Salads Like Mom Makes* T-shirts huddled around a single cell phone. They looked up to see Hubert standing there. They all took a second look at the phone.

There was a quick knock on another door. A tall thin guy, with no shortage of flamboyance, burst in. "Ladies, once again we need—" He stopped at the sight of Hubert.

One of the ladies took the phone and looked at it closer.

The tall guy held the door open for Hubert. His face was strangely inviting: creepy really. Reluctantly, Hubert went through. The tall guy grew a smile the Devil would appreciate.

"Careful there, Rand," the lady with the phone said.

"Shirley, please…" Rand closed the door, now alone with Hubert.

Hubert was clear from the Chinese chefs for sure, but who knew what this new guy had in mind. At least sharp objects were no longer an issue.

In this room, another thin guy, sporting a baker's hat

with an *Only Donut Holes* logo, stopped stacking trays of fresh donut holes when he saw Hubert. He checked his cell phone quickly.

Hubert was suddenly pulled out, but he had no idea by whom. He saw disappointment on Rand's face, but there was no attempt to keep Hubert here. Before the door closed, Hubert heard Rand flamboyantly say, "Well, he's *not* the only one, Danny."

Hubert almost tripped. He was pushed into a storage room. It was likely one of the Chinese madmen. The thought of the knives they were carrying returned. Now one of them had him alone in a room. *My God: that Tung guy... Why not the Mexican, Javier? Or even Abid, Rocco, or Tyrell. At least they weren't armed. A better choice would be Mark or Shirley. Even Rand beats a screaming Asian.* He turned, bordering on being terrified. It was Leigh with him.

"Your order's on the way, you're gonna have to pay," Leigh said in her bad Chinese accent. She oozed with happiness.

He'd forgotten about Leigh and all the other girls in the food court for that matter. He'd forgotten about his job, and Chester, and Rod. Will had been ecstatic... *about the picture.* But Leigh had him trapped in here, and it all came flooding back. *Oh, God, the picture...*

Hubert reacted by covering up. "Please... Please don't—I mean, I just—"

"You ready for that extra heat?"

Hubert hit Leigh with pleading eyes. Whatever she had planned with him, alone in this room, he wasn't ready for. Before this day started he was fine. He was unpopular, dorky, a loner; and that was just how Hubert wanted it. For some reason, all of that had suddenly changed. He wasn't able to process it this fast, if at all.

She was looking back at him, confused. "Or, was that your friend?"

"Will? Yes, it was Will. Me, definitely not."

"Really… Odd behavior at such a young age."

Hubert tried for an explanation. "It's just that… I'm not—"

"Ready, for responsibility beyond cleaning tables?"

Hubert didn't answer, but she couldn't have been more right. Will had put him up to this. This was Will's dream. For some reason, however, Hubert was the one living it.

Leigh continued, "It's your first day?

Hubert nodded.

"What's with the indoor track meet? Whatcha running from?"

"Everyone, everything," Hubert said. *Which, by the way, is so confusing to me right now, I couldn't even begin to explain other than saying, everyone, everything.*

"The picture?"

That's a good place to start…

"And now you," Hubert said.

Leigh appeared to be processing this. She shook her

head in frustration. "Relax, I don't serve poontang." She took her T-Woks hat and put it on Hubert's head. "I was just spreading a little hot sauce to watch you squirm."

She smiled. "Love what you do. That's me... Leigh."

The smile turned to guilt. "Sorry, but I had to save you from the crazies I work with. Believe me, I know how they can be when something stirs up their wok."

She didn't appear to be anything like the others in the food court, especially Virginia Almond. Hubert had already figured out how genuine she was. It was clearly coming from her eyes. Her voice was soothing and pleasant to listen to. He was fully aware of the connection between them even though it was thick with confusion.

The confusion didn't come from Leigh, however. It was all about what he would do now, outside this room. In here, she'd already calmed him down. He felt understood and protected. Even Will had never given Hubert that. But out there, there was a firestorm for him to face.

He would have to fight off the flaming hot chicks: a concept that still baffled him. Will would only fan those flames, and Leigh would probably run for the hills. *And it's all because of a picture? And my...* He shook his head, struggling to figure it all out.

Leigh found a pair of old sunglasses. She inspected them then handed them over.

Hubert put them on.

"There, disguised like the celebrity you've instantly

become," Leigh said with a warming smile.

Hubert smiled back with the confidence of a white mouse. "I can't go back."

Leigh stared him down. She shrugged with empathy. "Well, try again tomorrow. I can fix your man rod."

Hubert froze.

She looked at him, confused by his sudden reaction. "What? Your man... Supervisor... Rod," she said.

Hubert sighed with relief.

"Come on, I'll get you out from the rear."

Hubert was unsure again.

Leigh lifted an eyebrow. "Rear... door...

CHAPTER 5

Hubert stood motionless inside the front door of his moderate, suburban home. He leaned back, wide-eyed, as the door shut. He dropped his knapsack. It hit the floor with a thud. He stood in the foyer, shocked by the current disaster he now had to deal with.

He had time to think during his walk home alone. No one had seen him leave the shopping center. No screaming girls, sexed out on who knows what, chased him down; no enraged guys, looking to reclaim their lost popularity, cornered him. Even Will hadn't confused him into making decisions Hubert didn't want to make. But despite being alone and having the opportunity to clarify what had just happened, Hubert was no further ahead.

At least he was safe. As far as he knew, no one except Will would have any clue where he was now. This would give him more time to figure this out, but he suddenly realized it didn't matter how all this happened, or why. What mattered was how he was going to react. Certainly, his next appearance would have the same effect on the crazed girls, but he was not the type to capitalize. He preferred to hide, but he'd just done that. So the question was, *what's next?*

Of course, there was always the chance this would be a distant memory by tomorrow. How much impact could a simple picture have on a whole population of teenaged girls anyway? If they forget all about it, the guys definitely would too. So really, there was nothing to worry about. *Yeah, that's right.* He had escaped in the heat of the moment. From now on, it would be back to his mundane life, just like he wanted.

Before moving away from the door, he looked around realizing this was just where he needed to be to get himself back on track. The food court was too much for Hubert; working there was over the top. Now his popularity had soared there… *How could that possibly…?*

His father, Ralph, looked up from behind a huge, rolled up piece of carpet in the living room. "Hubert, quick, before this thing makes me thin again." His father fought to keep the roll tight.

Hubert's mother, Norma, appeared from another room. She jumped on the roll. "Oh, Ralph, really. Stop drowning in stupidity."

Suddenly, she lost interest in helping Ralph and bolted

for Hubert like a school girl would greet her puppy dog. "Ralph, look! Our little boy's back from the grind."

Her eyes beamed at Hubert. She stopped in front of him and pressed the janitor uniform he was still wearing as though she had clothes irons for palms.

Hubert hadn't thought about his mother's reaction after his first day of work, but he suddenly realized there was nothing he could do about her uncontrolled excitement. If he didn't have other things on his mind, he probably would have come up with a plan to avoid her. Actually, her affection wasn't bothering him all that much. At least her hands would touch nothing more than his clothes, and she was his mother after all.

Her sudden interest in him was probably doing his father a big favor too. It looked like renovations were underway, and his father would definitely be better off without her, *support*. Hubert looked beyond her at his father still struggling with the carpet. *But then again...*

***

Hubert walked with his father toward their van, parked crooked in the driveway. Hubert was concerned about how hyper his father was. First it had been the carpet, and now the van was of extreme urgency for some reason. After seeing the van, Hubert started to get the full picture. The erratic parking was one thing, but more importantly, the tires appeared ready to burst.

"They tried to upsell me delivery," his father said. He got to the van and hammered the wheel well. "Can you believe that? Do I look like an idiot, Hubert?" His father's confidence swelled. "I should drive it back just to prove a point."

Hubert stayed put as his father moved around to the back door. He knew what to expect when his father was like this because it happened often enough. Projects, vacations, movie night anticipating the newest blockbuster just released to video... Anything new could move this man into emotional turmoil. The sight of the van had Hubert's senses heightened. He squinted at the thought of what any movement might do.

"It's just a few boxes," his father said.

He pulled the latch. The door swooshed up. It scared the shit out of Hubert.

"Three-quarter inch, exotic tiger hardwood with nine coats of UV cured polyurethane and aluminum oxide," his father proudly continued.

Hubert's eyes popped when he saw the van filled floor-to-ceiling. He watched the invoice fall on the ground at his father's feet.

"I know, son. Your mother's idea. You know how she is when her juices get flowing." His father gave him a perverted look Hubert didn't want to see. "Better get to work. Wouldn't want to let that river dry up."

Hubert winced at the thought of that. His father whipped by, mentally ticking one item off his task list. Hubert was left with the daunting task of unloading.

***

Hubert lifted a box from the half-empty van. He was already worn out from the food court, but having his mind on something else was a welcome distraction. He turned away from the van, and he saw Will reluctantly riding up the driveway on a beat up BMX with a skipping pedal crank.

"Please don't tell me I'm gonna have to find a way to perform add-a-dick-to-me surgery," Will said.

Hubert thought about ignoring him, but what good would that do? He wouldn't be able to avoid Will's plans no matter how hard he tried, so he might as well hear what Will had in mind next. He put the box down on the driveway. "Can't you see I'm suffering enough here?" He went for another box.

"I swear, Pubes, I'll cut it off when you're sleepin' and use it as a strap-on if you're not gonna put it to good use."

Hubert looked back. He smiled a bit. "How ya gonna keep it up?"

"Mine from underneath can handle the load."

"So, you're going in with two?"

"Ya. Think they'll notice?"

They both laughed. There was one thing about Will that Hubert couldn't do without. It was his entertainment value. His plans may have been crazy, but he never took himself seriously. They could always laugh off the failures, and carry on to the next one. Hubert was fully aware of Will's intent to shift the line of fire away from himself, but having him around made every day an adventure to say the least. Without Will, Hubert's life as a teenager would be doomed.

"They might," Hubert said.

"Fuckin' sick, eh!"

"No, not sick..." Hubert paused to let Will catch up.

"DISEASED," they both shouted.

Will got off his bike as they both chuckled. He grabbed a box and checked out his flexed bicep for good measure. "Seriously though. You just got a silver platter full of Virginia, Her Hotness."

"All because they—she—whoever has seen my dick?"

"No, Pubes, of course not. Because the dick they saw was like none they've ever seen, or touched, or..." Will's eyes rolled back. "Why is this not happening to me?"

"So this is all about my uncut penis?"

"Combined with—you know what they say... *Abstinence makes the heart grow fonder.*"

"I don't think that's what they say."

"Probably not, but that's what we're going with."

"And that means?"

"That means, Pubes, the girls, the parties. That means your time has come. Our time…"

Hubert strained while he lifted out another box. Will rushed to help.

"You're workin' on a full load here, Pubes. Consider me your front line of hardware support."

Hubert sighed. His expression spoke volumes: *ready or not Hubert Rawlings*. With this guy for his best friend, shying away was simply not an option. And the idea of it all just going away… Once again, Will had come up with a plan, and Hubert was going to be the one to carry it out. Hubert couldn't shift the responsibility in some way. There was a physical component involved—Hubert's physical component—which up until now, he'd been perfectly happy dealing with on his own.

Hubert shook his head unsure of how to deal with this. His sudden surge in popularity was based on something only he had ever seen or touched. Why were others so interested in changing that? Will seemed determined to change that, but Hubert didn't want anything to do with playing the role of food court stud. He certainly wasn't ready for it.

The front door opened. "Hubert, your father's turning blue," Norma said. She ripped a devilish smile. "Hi, Will."

Hubert watched Will cringe. He knew Will was squirming at the simple thought of having to talk to her.

"Nice wood choice, Mrs. Rawlings," Will said

reluctantly. "I can tell, Pubes is impressed." He slapped Hubert on the back.

"Please, Will, his name is Hubert."

"She scares me, Pubes," Will whispered.

Hubert replied quietly, "Who do you think she'll scare if I show her off at the food court?"

Will's hands frantically waved in the air as if to erase that thought.

"She'll want to see where I work; meet my new friends." Hubert started toward the house with a box. "By the way, this is hardwood. Not hardware."

"Wood, ware… As long as it's hard," Will said.

Hubert turned back to him at the door and smiled slightly. He continued, struggling to get the box through the door.

CHAPTER 6

"Shit! Not again," Hubert said quietly to himself. His eyes were wide open, but it was too dark to make anything out in his room. He turned slightly to see his alarm clock glowing: *3:23*. He peeled back his covers, but he was careful not to move. He looked down just like so many times he had before. He couldn't see what he suspected. A slight touch of his crotch confirmed it.

He squirmed a little and shook his head with a sigh. His eyes were adjusting to the dark now. He sat up slowly and stayed on the side of his bed. He looked up to see his work clothes folded neatly on his desk. The T-Woks hat was on top.

He tried to convince himself that the reason he was sitting in semen stained boxers was simply because of the day's events. A guy like Will would be claiming this a victory. For Hubert, however, that wasn't the case. What had gone down at the food court had nothing to do with this for two reasons.

First, nothing about the food court incident was sexually motivating for him. If anything, it was terrifying. Okay, maybe the warrior princess—Leigh was her name—spiked his interest, but the dream had nothing to do with Leigh. It was about Virginia Almond, and what she'd been doing to him left him on the verge of panic.

She had him cornered in the same storage room he'd been in with Leigh. Unlike with Leigh, however, Virginia was determined to get a front row view of everything the now popular picture promised. Hubert cringed. *I can't believe there's actually a picture like that out there.* She had approached him slowly with tantalizing eyes that only looked at his crotch. He had tried to move, but he was frozen. She kept coming but never touched him. With every step closer, Hubert's panic heightened. She reached out but was always too far away. She took another step; she reached again. Hubert squirmed. She was too close. This would be the time she touched his… Then of course he woke up, and the result of that panic attack was left in his shorts and beginning to dry.

He shifted knowing he had to move soon, but he stayed there because the second reason bothered him more than the dream. These nightly adventures were happening way too often, he thought. If this had been the only one, then sure, he could attribute its occurrence to

Virginia Almond. But that wasn't the case. These dreams were like binge watching a porno series he starred in. He could only conclude they were a direct result of him not doing anything sexually when he was awake.

Maybe Will's insistence to become more popular was a direct message to get on with this puberty thing. Maybe the picture was just what Hubert needed to kick start his motivation. Maybe Will had a good point... *I'm the wearer of the golden sleeve.* Maybe, Will was having the same type of dreams. He was just more determined: one step ahead in finding a solution.

He got up and pulled at the front of his boxers. He went to his dresser and opened the top drawer. This was nothing but routine for Hubert.

***

The bathroom door opened, and Hubert walked across the hallway, disappearing into his room.

Norma watched him from the shadows. She knew exactly what had just happened to Hubert. She was prepared for it every night. An internal alarm went off for Norma after her son's fire burned. She was determined to give him space, though, and not to embarrass him with a confrontation. After all, it wasn't his fault. She was responsible for all her son was going through.

Actually, it was Ralph's fault, she thought. He had

insisted Hubert be just like him. Ralph was the one who had convinced her it was the right thing to do, despite what the doctors were saying. She shook her head and looked down.

She sighed, remembering that event so many years ago. She had suspected back then that Hubert would somehow be affected by her lack of knowledge on the topic, but she never suspected this result. The doctor's had talked about cleanliness. Ralph had simply laughed off that logic. Sensitivity had never come up as an issue by anyone. Her decision had been based only on what Ralph said. He was her husband: the father of their newborn son. Who else should she have trusted when it came down to the decision about circumcision? She should have known better...

She looked back up. She saw Hubert's closed door. She waited silently for a few seconds then carefully walked toward the bathroom.

CHAPTER 7

Hubert stood at his bedroom window looking aimlessly outside. It was as though the events from yesterday had just happened. Awkward moments usually lost their intensity over time with Hubert, but not this catastrophe. His hope was that it would all just go away, but he doubted that it would work out that way. Now, he was only a few hours away from having to face it all again.

The reality of it was definitely still there, especially with Will in his cheering section. This sudden realization that he was running out of time made him think about how he should try to make the best of it. That was scary for Hubert, though. He wasn't the type of person who responded well to sexual advances. In fact, he'd never had any sexual opportunities, so this was definitely new chartered territory for him. Even with Will close by as his mentor, a drastic personality change was something he didn't think he was capable of.

He could go back there, however, and simply do his job. If he promised himself that the back rooms of the food court were out of bounds, he could probably keep his head down and stay busy enough. Eventually, everyone should ignore him if he ignored them. He didn't know if that would be enough to avoid this mess, but without another plan...

His only other option would be to tackle this head on. He shuddered at the thought of that, but it was something he couldn't afford to ignore. The choice may not be his to make. This could quite possibly be the only way.

The personality change would be his biggest obstacle, but he just needed to take control really. *That's what Will would do. Find your inner rock star, Hubert Rawlings. It just might work.*

He looked back to his desk; his uniform and the T-Woks hat. He went there and opened the lid on his laptop.

***

In the middle of the kitchen, Ralph put down the armchair he had carried in from the living room. He postured like the rock he wasn't then looked for a reaction. Norma wasn't looking. He turned away with wrinkled lips. A little deflated, he headed back to the living room.

"It can't stay there," Norma said. She continued at the sink.

Ralph stopped. That woman has eyes in the strangest places, he thought. "A man needs motivation to keep him inspired." He crafted up his idea of a sexy smile.

Norma ignored him. She didn't turn around. She had no acknowledgment, no smile: nothing. "Find your own inspiration."

Those were hard words for a guy just trying to keep things calm, but her saucy bitch attitude wasn't enough to stop him now. He slid forward and took hold of her from behind. He knew what was bugging her so much, and it had nothing to do with furniture in the kitchen. Well, that probably didn't help, but this was something he could easily take care of with his charm, he thought. "Quick, in the kitchen, before the boy gets up," he whispered in her ear.

Norma pushed away, disgusted. "Ralph, grow up! That's the last thing Hubert needs to see."

Ralph stepped back quickly with his hands up. He'd been in this situation before—too many times actually. He knew the signs; he shouldn't have even tried. He turned away and took the rejection well. "Might do him some good."

***

Hubert stopped before entering the bathroom. It had been quiet in his room, but now that he was in the hallway, he could hear what sounded like the beginning of his parents squaring off on each other. He listened carefully, hearing his mother.

"Well, at least I'm big enough to admit we've made a mistake."

"Norma, please stop with the melodrama. Everything's fine."

"No, Ralph, it's not fine. You can't just stand there pretending that the world's perfect."

Hubert looked confused. He didn't know of anything wrong between them. Maybe it was just about some renovation decision they'd made. It wouldn't be strange for his mother to be freaking out about something like that, and his father would no doubt try to brush it off. He headed back to his bedroom.

"But your psycho-diagnosis is wrong, Norma."

"It's not wrong, and there's a way to solve it."

"Norma, Norma. Nothing drastic, please."

Nothing drastic… Please tell me she's not going over the top on color selection or accessories. Hubert continued to his desk and grabbed a set of headphones.

Back in the hallway, he began to put them on, but…

"I'm not willing to live like this. This is our son we're talking about. I'm concerned…"

Hubert could tell Norma had started to cry. He also

knew this was about him, not trim options.

"Something must be done."

***

Ralph slid the armchair across the floor. "What you're talking about is completely unfair." He'd been packing the kitchen with furniture, but now his mind was only thinking about stopping Norma from tipping over the edge.

"But necessary. In the long run, Ralph, it's better this way."

He stopped in front of her. He grabbed her shoulders. "Norma, listen to me. You have no idea about any of this. It's a guy thing. Just let it be, Norma." He gave her the most genuine look he could come up with. "Trust me, dear. Hubert's gonna be just fine."

She paused for a second. At first, Ralph thought he'd gotten through to her. He was right about her backing off. She had no business planning things like this or taking action for that matter. Then she blinked and turned away sharply.

"I already trusted you on this. Now I get to make the decisions," she said sternly.

Ralph knew right then he'd lost his only chance with her. He had his face-to-face, but now there was no stopping her. "No, Norma, no! I'm not listening to this."

He grabbed an I-Pod from the counter.

***

Hubert sat at his desk in boxers and with his headphones on. The closed door almost guaranteed him against any parental conflict or distraction. Even though his parents had been arguing about him, he had no intention to get involved. He had other problems to deal with, and the clock was ticking toward what he would do next.

He opened his email program. He was shocked!

His inbox was full of Facebook invitations. The only invitations he'd ever gotten were from creepy people, so this was unusual in a good way. He scrolled through them and stopped at a note from Will. He opened it.

The only thing in the message was pictures of Virginia. They were sexy, provocative. There were school shots, and posing shots; pictures of her dancing, partying, and making out. She was younger in some and just as she was now in others.

Hubert wondered how Will got all these pictures, and how long he'd had them. Has his best friend been creeping Virginia Almond for years? Regardless, it was a fine collection and for his eyes only.

He noticed action under his boxers.

***

Norma worked at the counter, frustrated beyond belief. Some time had passed since her argument with Ralph, and she hadn't seen him since. That was just as well, she thought. The last thing she needed now was his damned ideas blocking her way.

She turned to a cupboard and backed into another chair Ralph had dumped off here. She kicked it, but it went nowhere. She climbed over a sofa to get out of a kitchen that was now packed like a moving van with a sink.

She managed to move into the hallway where she had to squeeze past boxes of hardwood, stacked against both walls. She looked into a totally empty living room. She covered her eyes while shaking her head. She didn't know how much longer she could take it with her house like this.

She heard the shower start from upstairs. She headed for the stairs. "Hubert, make it quick in there. You have work soon," she yelled.

She thought her trip up the stairs would include another confrontation with Ralph. He was no longer downstairs, so he must be up there. She continued to the top without seeing Ralph. That was a good thing, she thought. If she was lucky, she would make it all the way to her bedroom, leaving Ralph a distant memory for now.

***

Norma did the final touches on her designer bed. She looked around, content with perfection. With the door closed and Ralph nowhere in sight, she was noticeably more relaxed here. It wasn't likely to last, but for now she cherished the moment. Compared to the kitchen, this was Norma's Heaven.

This time away gave her a moment to think. Her decision was clear now. She wasn't thinking about herself or any of Ralph's reservations. Sure, Ralph should be able to understand these male things better than her, but it was *Ralph's* opinion she was having to rationalize. She'd learned over the years how that wasn't a good thing to do. This was all about what was best for Hubert, and she was confident her decision was the right one. At least in the long run...

She checked a clock and suddenly panicked. The shower was still running.

She burst into the hallway. Norma beelined for the bathroom and stopped at a closed door. "Hubert—"

"I'm leaving."

She heard that from downstairs. She turned away from the door but only for a second.

"You have work!" Norma continued as if shouting at the bathroom door.

"See ya!"

She turned away again, frustrated. "Ralph, just wait." She turned back to the door. "Hubert, you're going to be late."

There was no response from the bathroom. The shower kept running.

"Where are you going, Ralph?"

There was no response from downstairs either.

"Hubert, it's only your second day." She tried the handle. It turned. She swung the door open. "Hubert!"

Her eyes popped.

"Ralph!"

Ralph's eyes were closed. His earbuds were in. His hand moved to the unheard beat. He was smiling. He was swaying. He was...

"Ralph! My God, Ralph, you're masturbating."

He heard that.

CHAPTER 8

Will stood in front of T-Woks, poised with forced posture, as though *his* show was about to begin. He was well aware this was not about him, but his best friend would soon make an appearance. For Will, that was good enough. Pubes had already made it perfectly clear he was in way over his head, so if anyone should be there to pick up his pieces, it should be Will. He smiled huge at that thought and straightened up more. *I am his best friend after all.*

Will had a chance to capitalize yesterday. That had been the opportunity of his lifetime, and he crumbled under all that passionate pressure. Will closed his eyes just thinking about it. He scolded himself for not being able to control Pubes, but it had all come on so quick. Before he knew it, Pubes was gone and Will had been left there with Virginia Almond within arm's reach. His arms didn't reach, though.

His mouth stayed closed. He didn't twitch, blink, scratch, or even take a breath. He remembered being basically immobilized by the goddess's close presence.

But everything was different now. A whole day had passed, and Will was ready to make up for lost time. He had planned his whole teenaged life for an event like this, and his best friend was about to pull it off. Well, Pubes would likely screw it up, but Will was there. This time he was prepared for the role he had to play. *Consider me your front line of hardware support.* He'd said that to Pubes yesterday, and he was here today to make sure all the poles stayed in the air. Hopefully, at the end of the day, his pole would be the last one standing.

He looked around the food court at the standing room only crowd. Will had never seen a shortage of activity here, but this time it was like a cafeteria on pause despite the overwhelming attendance. Most of the customers were female. Store owners were poised and ready for business, but no one was buying. No one was moving. Everyone anticipated, like *surprise* would be the next word out of their mouths.

He looked back to see that stern Tung guy standing at the cash register behind T-Woks' counter. Eye contact frightened Will, so he looked away quickly. He saw the Chinese chefs waiting with their knives ready. This had been the same scene Pubes faced yesterday, and he would likely crumble if he had to go through it again. Will was here to direct traffic, so he would have to be sure the chefs stayed clear.

A girl appeared from behind Will. He jumped a bit, ruining his bid for best postured man. "I doubt he's ready for such a performance," she said.

Will remembered her: the T-Woks girl with the bad accent, Leigh. He remembered her being there when Pubes jumped the counter. From that point on, though, Will didn't know what happened to Pubes, or Leigh for that matter. He looked at her curiously. "How do you know...?" Will thought it through for a second. "Did you rescue him?"

Leigh smiled him the answer.

Will shook his head slightly. *Maybe my man Pubes has got this...* Will looked back to the seating area. "The boy's gonna sizzle." He kept looking straight ahead, straight toward the door by the washrooms. Straight at the beginning of the best day of his teenaged life.

Finally, the door cracked open. There was hesitation. The area went deadly quiet. Will noticed that all eyes were on the door, then it opened wide. The crew reluctantly entered their arena. Chester came in last, but he looked like he was wishing he hadn't. Everyone was disappointed, including Will, until Pubes appeared in the doorway.

He had shades on. A T-Woks hat was in place and tilted to the side. Elvis had arrived.

***

Hubert stepped away from the door but paused before going any further. He waited until the rest of the crew had dispersed themselves into the crowd. His intention going into this was to just be one of those guys, but that idea quickly changed from the reaction he'd gotten in the locker room.

Obviously, they had experienced nothing but rejection since yesterday's event. When Hubert had arrived in the locker room their resentment was clear. Their reaction to him had been cold and bitter. Because of that, he'd been forced to make a choice. He could cower in the corner and let them have their popularity back, or he could rise above them and take it all for himself. He chose the latter; although, there would still be the issue of him, Hubert *Pubes* Rawlings, having to pull it off.

Hubert stepped into the food court and suddenly, there was energy, like the lights had just surged. He strode to a table with a wet and dry cloth in hand. If he had taken time to think about it, he probably would have failed, but he rode that pony. He cleaned like a magician. Girls melted nearby.

His plan now was to keep his head down and work, but he was on stage and dressed for the part. He remembered how the rest of the crew worked this crowd. Although he had no tricks up his sleeve, he had something down his pants that seemed to be of interest. That interest kept all eyes on him, so all he could do was play it up the best he could.

When he moved to another table, the girls nearby gave him space. They moved away shyly: timid because of being close to him. He looked up to get a clear view of all his supporters. He was shocked by the numbers and that he was still keeping their interest. So far, all was good for Hubert with his sudden leap into fame. *Just stay focused and clean. This is going to be a snap.*

Although the girls near him seemed harmless, others deeper in the crowd appeared more aggressive. He focused on them while he moved to another table. He made eye contact with one. She seemed to be in attack mode. Others beside her were the same.

A sudden chill broke his confidence. He should have worked harder with the crew before coming here. These girls seemed ready to pounce, and he didn't stand a chance against them out here on his own. He needed the crew to cover for him, but they were nowhere to be seen.

Hubert looked toward T-Woks. Leigh was serving a customer, but she was watching him. Her welcoming smile was infectious and gave him some of that spirit back. He lost himself in her attractiveness until Virginia stood up and blocked his view.

His courage faded. A shade of panic started to take over. The girls he'd seen before now flanked her. Hubert's bid for stardom was about to elevate, and he was alone. He needed a solution quick. He turned back to the door. He could run back there and cower in the basement, but that would be just like he'd done before. Doing that again wouldn't solve anything, so he needed to keep up with his show and move this thing forward.

All he had to do was get away from the aggressive ones, but they were moving now, straight toward him. The tables weren't enough protection. He needed to get away from the table area. Any one of the food vendors would give him refuge, but going there would still leave him vulnerable.

He looked around frantically: tables, chairs, neon food logos, and people looking at him. He saw Will near T-Woks, and he was alone. Of course Will was alone, he thought. Even among all this weirdness happening, Will was still Will, and he would be alone.

Will definitely was his out.

CHAPTER 9

Hubert stepped into his house and closed the front door. It was loud in here, but that didn't concern him much. Home was where he wanted to be—where he needed to be. Once again he was safe, which was more important than the background noise of indoor construction.

It had been a long shift and tense at times, but a whole day in the food court had definitely dulled some of the fascination with his unclipped dick. He sighed and shook his head still struggling with why, and how, all this had happened.

When he'd made his way over to T-Woks, where Will had been, all the attention toward Hubert had suddenly diminished. Even though everyone stayed, and Hubert still had to deal with prying eyes and hushed conversations, the Virginia squad stopped their desperate pursuit. That was enough to calm everyone down, and Hubert had room to breathe. Will had stepped up to capture some of the attention, and that pretty much sealed the deal to keep the admirers away.

Because of that, Hubert made a quick decision to keep Will close. He would have preferred to have the crew doing that dirty work, but Will had done fine. Will was in his moment. He desperately tried to capture the attention for himself, but all he really did was clear a path for Hubert to move around. Will had been relentless and stayed with Hubert the whole time.

At the end of the shift, Will was exhausted. Hubert was too, but the success of the day was something he cherished. Now he leaned against the door. He closed his eyes, but not for long...

His mother was right there to greet him, again. She said something, but hammering drowned her out. Hubert just then became fully aware of the noise in here. It was overwhelming and involved his father and the hardwood. Judging by the look on his mother's face, however, the noise was probably a good thing. At least he didn't have to hear her.

She was clearly dragged down and frustrated, but she managed to find an octave above the racket. "Stop that damned banging, Ralph!"

His father looked up from the living room. He was silent for a second, then he looked away. A power drill rang out.

His mother shouted louder, "And that!"

His father turned back to them, impatiently. The drill stopped. He didn't even look at Norma. His eyes went straight to Hubert. Hubert could see from the strain on his face that something was up which had nothing to do with accurate measurements or the micro-beveled appearance of hardwood planks. Suddenly his father's eyes softened. He looked at Hubert as if to say, *poor bastard.*

At this point Hubert didn't know what to think. He watched his father turn away defeated, obviously by his mother. She still stood in Hubert's way. She had him pinned from going any further. He tried, but she would have none of that. Whatever the problem was between these two, Hubert would soon be included.

His mother took his hand. Without saying anything, she led him toward the kitchen. Reluctantly, he followed. He looked to his father for some type of reaction, but he was pretending to be preoccupied. Hubert wished his mother would just insist he help his father, but that didn't appear to be what this was about. Her persistence led him down the hallway.

In the kitchen, he saw it was less congested than the last time he'd been here, but it was still decorated like a living room. He had trouble finding anywhere to go. His mother struggled to find her way to the counter too, so he turned to leave. This probably had something to do with him helping to get this stuff out of here. After the shift he'd just gone through, the last thing he wanted was to do handiwork with his parents. His only chance was to get away while she was distracted.

His mother didn't let him get any distance on her, though. "Sit down, Hubert. Your father and I—"

Hubert tried to resist, but his mother insisted he sit in the armchair. *Well, at least I'm not lifting it out of here.*

"Just for the record, son, I did all I could," his father said as he came into the room from another entrance.

"Ralph, please. There's no bad guy here."

His mother sat on the arm of the sofa, close to Hubert.

"It's for the best, dear. Trust me," she said.

Hubert's reaction was immediate. "What's for the best?" He'd been left in the dark too long, and he didn't like where this seemed to be going. "Don't tell me you guys—"

His father turned away. "I tell ya, Norma, it's a mistake. The boy can't take it. How can we expect him to deal with this?"

"Take what? Deal with what?"

His mother took Hubert's hand. "Dear, your father and I…" She looked to his father for support. She got none. "We feel it's best that we take action against our little problem." She paused with a concerned look, obviously hoping Hubert would catch on. "It's all about sensitivity, dear." She lit up like suddenly everything was okay. "We clear that up and—"

Hubert pulled away from her. "Listen, you guys are freakin' me out. Just friggin' come out with it."

"Hubert!"

His mother reached for him caringly, but Hubert would have none of that nurturing stuff.

"Norma, if it's gonna be this way, then it's done. He's right dammit. Tell him," his father said.

His mother looked away.

His father looked the other way.

Hubert looked worried.

"Hubert..." His mother glanced at his father. "I certainly don't want you to do like Daddy does."

"Sorry, son," his father said as reassuringly as he could.

His mother looked him square in the eyes. He tried to blink her stare away, but it didn't work.

"You're going to be circumcised, dear," she continued.

It was dead quiet after that. Hubert shifted restlessly. "I'm going to be what?"

Again, there was nothing but complete silence.

His mother repeated, "Circumcised—"

That's what I thought you said. Hubert pounced up from the chair, but his mother's piercing stare sat him back down again. "At seventeen? Are you f—" He tried to shake this all out of his head. "Nuts?"

"Watch yourself, son." His father gave Hubert his stern warning face. "So far, she's not touching those."

He watched his mother stare his father down with lead-loaded eyeballs.

Hubert grabbed his head with both hands. He looked up to the ceiling then back to his parents with eyes like surgical lights. He tried for some type of argument, but he could see the determination in his mother's eyes.

There was nothing he could do. He knew his mother well enough. She was simply a control freak, and she always stuck to her decisions: just like she had him pinned down here and glued to this chair.

His father didn't stand a chance in changing her mind either. Hubert was sure he'd tried, but his father's approach with his mother was usually, *let it ride*. His life was easier that way, especially with issues that didn't directly concern him.

The bottom line was, his mother had made a decision. Hubert *Pubes* Rawlings was going to be circumcised at seventeen. There would be nothing more to discuss except who was going to do the cutting.

CHAPTER 10

Hubert lay on an operating table, alone in this completely sterile room. The whole process of how he ended up here left him feeling cold and abandoned, the same way he felt lying helpless on this table. How could she possibly think anything good would come from this? His father; the doctors. Didn't anyone try talking some sense into her?

After the eventful announcement his mother had forced on him, she moved swiftly into action, pushing him to this final resting place. Her drive and determination—an obsession really—to get this done had left his head spinning. It was only now that he had a chance to breathe, but every breath he took felt like it should be his last.

It was like he was strapped down, but nothing held him here. He didn't dare move, though. Just the thought of the embarrassment his mother could cause if he put up any type of fight sent shockwaves racing through his head. That, combined with the fear of what was coming, pinned him to this table as though he was a corpse.

He remembered his mother dodging around stranded strips of hardwood and opened boxes with her ear glued to a cell phone. She'd maneuvered herself over furniture placed in the strangest places. Hubert had tried to interrupt those conversations and get his point across to her. He didn't need any circumcision, he had insisted, but she didn't hear any of what he had to say. She only cared about the phone back then. The information she'd got from listening to that was her ticket to putting Hubert right where he was now.

He looked to his right at monitoring equipment in front of a white, subway tiled wall. To his left was an empty floor stand and cabinets with clear glass doors. He tried to focus on the stuff in the cabinets, but he was too messed up to figure out what any of it would be used for. The floor stand was there for him. It was empty now, but soon that wouldn't be the case. He cringed thinking what that thing would be holding when this was all over.

He closed his eyes and decided to just look straight ahead. He was ashamed of himself for not being able to put up a convincing defense. He should be making his own decisions, especially about things like this. This was the same problem he had with Will, and look at the mess Will had gotten him into. He sighed with the thought of his gutlessness. He needed to change this—take things into his own hands. He sighed again. Just the thought of that, and what was about to happen, made him shiver. *And exactly why is it that all this is about my penis: the one thing only I should have access to?*

He didn't want to open his eyes because he'd already seen what was there. Possibly, just waiting this out with his eyes closed was best. After a few seconds, he opened them anyway. He was forced to look at a distorted image of himself in the huge surgical lamps that dominated the ceiling.

A nurse walked into the room followed by another. He could see them from the corner of his eye, but he had no intentions of making eye contact with them. They knew what he was here for. They would no doubt smile and make him feel comfortable, but he knew what all the smiling was really about. They both probably had to take a minute at the door to control their hysterics before entering.

Suddenly, the door opened again. Damn, Hubert thought. The whole staff seemed to be settling in to enjoy the show for their break. Soon he would see them gather around with coffee and danishes. He panicked not remembering if the procedure was actually scheduled for twelve noon. "*Oh, look, you brought donuts,*" he thought he heard someone say. He closed his eyes again realizing if they didn't get on with this thing soon, he would simply shrivel up like a crazed lunatic right here on the table. He opened his eyes and looked at the nurses. *They didn't actually have donuts did they?*

Hubert turned away from the nurses and his whole body jumped at the sight of the surgeon standing at the other side of the table. His surgical mask was only hanging around his neck, so Hubert could see his sarcastic smile. *Okay, he's a professional. It's just a smile...*

"You know, Hubert, I could have done this general, but your mother insisted on local." He turned, holding up a larger than life syringe. "You're a tough dude."

Hubert knew the look on his face said otherwise. It was one thing when he had been alone in here, but now all the players had hit the floor. Desperation flooded him then he realized again that he wasn't tied down. He looked at his arms and hands, all free to move anyway he wished. *Why is that? You're going to cut me down there when I'm free to move around...* He looked at the surgeon with pleading eyes. *Please, strap me to this board. Please hit me, or gas me, or pump something into me to stop this from happening... And, please, stop listening to my mother.*

"Well, imagine the story you'll have for your friends," the surgeon continued without looking at Hubert.

Friends, what friends? I have no friends... Just Will and... My God! The food court. Throughout all the buildup that had put him on this table, he'd completely forgotten about the food court. He was basically a celebrity there. It was just what he needed, but that was only because of... He looked down at his crotch. He shook his head realizing how messed up everything was for him now.

Hubert turned back to the surgeon while he laid the syringe on the tool tray next to another one. Shock filled Hubert's face knowing those were going to be used on him. The surgeon looked at Hubert with another smile.

There, you just saw the look on my face. Surely, you're not going through with it after seeing that.

"Just think of it as a bad haircut."

Apparently, the look of desperation was something this guy had seen before, Hubert thought. *My face... Don't you see I'm freaking out here?* Hubert watched the surgeon hold up a sterile bag of circumcision tools. He pulled on it tight.

"A week from now you won't feel a thing." The surgeon smiled again.

Now that is a sarcastic smile...

The surgeon cut clean through the plastic.

CHAPTER 11

Hubert noticed he was in the same storage room he'd been in with Leigh. Once again, he wasn't with Leigh, though. He was with Virginia.

The room was different from how he'd remembered it. It was definitely the storage room, but it reminded him of his bedroom. That was just a fleeting thought, however. He had Virginia Almond in here, so why would he care if he could see the T-Woks hat on his desk?

She had that determined look on her face again. She approached, but this time Hubert wasn't frozen. She kept coming, and Hubert did nothing to stop her. He anticipated her movements toward him—her aggression; her desperation. He welcomed it and moved his hips to entice her. Her eyes were focused on his crotch, and she seemed mesmerized from what she saw.

Hubert tried to look down, but he was unable to. He

didn't need to, though. She'd found what she was determined to see, and she certainly didn't need any help with what she was about to do. He did nothing to hide or cover himself up. This time Hubert was in full control, and power seemed to flow from his fingertips.

Virginia stepped closer. He could touch her if he wanted to. He spread out his fingers on both hands, but he touched nothing—not Virginia; not himself. Hubert moaned; he smiled. He closed his eyes knowing Virginia was going down, and he was rising to the occasion...

Suddenly, he launched straight up in his bed with his eyes wide open. "Ahhhhhhhhhhhhhhhhhhhhhhhhhhh!"

CHAPTER 12

"Remember this?"

Leigh looked up slightly from her paper plate filled with Shanghai Noodles. With her fork filled up, she wondered what Elle was talking about, and what she'd found on her phone. It must have been something really special if it could stop Elle from her annoying, repetitive scrolling.

Leigh continued eating since she figured it couldn't be all that important. Nothing coming from Elle ever was. Usually, things that sparked Elle's attention—and Jane's too for that matter—didn't do much for Leigh, but she spent a lot of time with these two, especially here at the food court. She often wondered why, though. She didn't mind being with them all that much, it was just that they were both so damned negative.

Leigh wasn't like that at all. She always saw the bright

side and did whatever she could to lighten things up. At T-Woks she had to deal with a grumpy owner and cranky chefs, not to mention the customers who all seemed to be having a bad day. She usually tried to do anything to cheer people up even if she was only successful at amusing herself. This wasn't always the case with Elle and Jane, though. For some reason, they could drag her down with their pessimism, and today was looking like she would likely join in if she stayed with them too long.

Jane's interest perked up instantly when she saw what Elle was looking at: a convenient distraction from the plate of mixed vegetables Elle and Jane shared. Leigh could see a gossip moment coming. The look on both their faces told Leigh to leave now before their attitudes caused her to gag on a mouthful of noodles.

"Oh, God, the dick pic. How did the *Bitches* possibly get over such a poor performance?"

While Jane said that, Leigh's attention had shifted from the two girls in front of her, to exactly who Jane was referring to as the *Bitches*. They had a whole section of the food court practically reserved for them: probably five tables total, all centered around Virginia Almond. No girls other than the Bitches ever went there, and the hot maintenance crew catered to their every need. The Bitches baited those guys and probably paid them off to keep them close by.

All that attention seeking disgusted Leigh, but they

definitely seemed better off than she was. They were more popular at least. She knew all the guys, especially Chester, but she would never do what the Bitches did, so the guys kept their distance. She couldn't be like the Bitches, and being one of them was completely out of the question.

They appeared to offend Elle and Jane too, but Leigh thought she could see right through those two. Elle and Jane were too much like the Bitches, but they had never been accepted in that group. Because of that, they despised them. They criticized them, but they knew everything the Bitches did and were never too far away from them.

Leigh could do without all of it, but she didn't want to be a loner. Elle and Jane were friends despite their different personalities, and she needed them. If it wasn't for all that negativity, she thought. She turned her attention back to her plate of noodles and her lunch partners. She watched Jane take a small bottle of hand sanitizer from her purse.

Elle dropped her phone on the table. "I'm sure Virginia Almond's claw marks left the loser scarred for life."

Leigh hadn't thought about the guy in the picture for a while, but his desperate face looking straight at her from Elle's phone was an extremely persistent reminder. She wondered what had become of that guy. He had a job here. So did she, but she hadn't seen him.

She liked what she'd seen in him. He was scared and

naive, but he wasn't hiding anything. From what little she knew about him, she doubted he was capable of operating with the hidden agendas everyone around here did.

She remembered his friend who was obsessed with all the attention coming from the picture. He was frantic really. Both of them were. They were the type Leigh seemed to always navigate toward. She didn't know what the attraction was. Maybe she felt she could help them fit in, but she didn't do that well herself. Maybe she didn't see any other choice since the Bitches were out of bounds. Maybe these two guys reminded her of herself...

They weren't a lot different than the three of them actually. They were all trying to find a way to fit into this teenaged battle ground. The maintenance crew ran the show here. The Bitches fueled them, and everyone else watched from the sidelines. In Leigh's case, the viewing area was a distant food court table that could really use some cleaning.

Maybe that was why Rod had that guy working here. After all, someone needed to look after the wannabes. Leigh knew Rod well enough. He was just the type to make sure everyone got their piece of the food court pie. After that guy's initial performance, however, Rod probably assigned him away from the food court. She shook away that thought and looked up.

Standing at a kiosk beyond the food court, she saw the desperate friend. She struggled to remember his name.

The maintenance crew fugitive had said it in the storage room after her *extra heat* comment. She couldn't come up with it, but it didn't matter anyway.

Jane asked, "Antiseptic, Leigh?"

Leigh suddenly shook her head. She wasn't really saying *no*. The head shake just brought her back to realizing she was actually sitting with people.

Jane fired off a disgusted look and turned to Elle for approval. "Eww, after handling all that money. Do you have any idea how many germs lurk around a place like this?"

"Let me know when you see my skin peeling," Leigh said. *There's that gloom again, not that my response was any better.*

Leigh saw Jane look at a smudge of food on the table. She cringed. Then she saw the picture again. She pushed the phone away. "I just can't look at it. Can you imagine how unsanitary that thing must be?"

I hadn't thought about it all that much, Jane. Actually, not at all. I'm surprised you'd actually care... But this was exactly the problem Leigh had with these two. They just seemed to dig way too deep to find anything to complain about.

Suddenly, Virginia swooshed by their table with the Bitches following.

"And she was just dying to clean up with it," Jane continued.

Well, that's true. Virginia had found a new trophy: something no one else had. Because of that, all the Bitches wanted him. But Leigh had met the guy involved, and he'd admitted it himself: *he wasn't ready for Virginia Almond.* She remembered him in the storage room, and he certainly wasn't. He wasn't ready for her or any of them for that matter.

Leigh studied Virginia then she looked back to the kiosk and Will was still there. She smiled at herself for suddenly remembering his name. These two definitely needed her help, especially if the other guy intended on coming back here. If nothing else, she knew the crew, and they controlled this place. She knew how these two should act, but she didn't know if she could deflect all the attention away from the popular appendage.

Once again, Leigh found herself sympathizing with the weak, but it energized her knowing a new project loomed. It was motivating, and it gave her an excuse to get away from Elle and Jane for a bit.

She kept watching Will knowing she would have to get to him if she was to find out more about the mysterious closet guy. That shouldn't be too hard, she thought. After all, he seemed pretty interested in what he was looking at which he shouldn't be. Especially considering his age and the fact that he was a guy...

CHAPTER 13

Will was completely preoccupied at the kiosk while he admired a small skin care sample. The food court was right beside him. That's where he had fully intended to spend his afternoon, but the sample caught his attention so everything else would have to wait. He had no great plans anyway. He was here alone and only came hoping he could benefit if Pubes was working.

He smoothed out the sample to get a clear view of what attracted him to it. He was shocked that he didn't know about the cocktail of remedies concealed in this little beauty. He usually stayed informed of the latest innovations in skin care, but every now and then something slipped past him. He turned it over. *What magic have they come up with now?*

He noticed the kiosk owner watching him closely under a Beautiful Brilliance store sign. This wasn't the first time

Will and this man had exchanged glances. He made Will nervous, and Will knew he should leave. He caught a glimpse of the food court, but this prize had him mesmerized. It was just a sample—his for the taking, he thought. He could grab as many as he wanted, but the creepy owner seemed to think otherwise. He should probably just put it down and move on, but the soft, pudgy little packet felt like part of him now. His collection simply couldn't do without it.

"Your boy's sizzle, fizzle."

Will jumped. It felt like his heart just flipped. *What the—who...* He hid the sample. "Fuck me!" He tried for a graceful recovery but dropped the sample instead. "That creepy accent again."

He spun around to see Leigh smiling at the sight of the sample. *Was she just looking down, or did she catch me in the act of enhancing my beauty knowledge?* Most likely the latter, but he didn't want her picking it up to confirm that.

Will tried to ignore the sample. The last thing he needed was the word getting out about his obsession with skin care products. He looked around nervously, but he couldn't help seeing it stranded and all alone. He'd just had it in his caring hands, but it seemed light years away now. All he needed to do was bend over and get it back, but he couldn't do that.

Leigh asked, "Yours?"

"Ummm..." Will looked down. "Oh that." He made

like it was nothing. He sighed and closed his eyes. When he opened them, he saw many of the same samples displayed on the kiosk. He couldn't have them either.

Leigh stepped in closer, right on the sample.

Will cringed. He almost collapsed actually. He wanted to fall to his knees and try to salvage whatever he could, but he didn't have time to deal with his emotional turmoil. Leigh was right there, inches from his face.

"Man, you have nice skin. No grey dull undertones. Nice hydration." She pinched his forehead. "You're a collagen heavyweight."

Will soaked up the compliments. It didn't make up for his current grief, but it was making things easier. No one had ever commented about his perfect complexion before. She had noticed, and she seemed to know what it took to get it that way.

Leigh wiped her foot. "Must be the food you eat."

No, food has nothing to do with it. She didn't know what Will did. His knowledge was clinical based; hers was *natural.* He saw the smudge Leigh left on the ceramic. It was just like road kill to him. He cringed knowing that a few hours from now, it would only exist on the soles of Beautiful Brilliance customer's shoes.

He looked back at the guilty one. She had turned away and was looking at the food court. "I should introduce you to my friends."

He saw the table she was looking at. The two girls he'd

seen her with before sat there. They were huddled together, infatuated with a cell phone. It was odd to Will placing Leigh with these two, but hey, what did he know about relationships between girls.

"I'm sure they wouldn't approve though," Leigh said.

"Approve of what?"

She looked back at him. "It's a social thing." She shook her head slightly. "A girl has to have standards," she said with a shoulder shrug and an eye twitch. "Hey, where's what's-his-name been?"

"Pubes?" *That's a damn good question…*

Leigh laughed question marks. "Okay, Pubes." She looked away slightly. "You really call him Pubes?"

"Yeah. His name's Hubert. Rhymes with puberty. Cut short for special effect."

"Creative."

Will took in that praise too. *Pubes* was his idea. It was intended to boost their popularity but never had much of an effect. Will had called him *Pubes* ever since the insightful day he'd come up with it, but he was the only one who did. Pubes's mother hated it, and Will didn't think Pubes liked being called *Pubes* either. He was mostly called by his real name, *Hubert*. Actually, most people didn't call him anything at all. Most people didn't call either of them by any name.

But now Will was standing at the edge of the food court talking to someone who looked like they—*she*—

actually cared. He postured up after realizing that and completely forgot about the skin care product. It was hard for Will to feel comfortable around Leigh, however. This chick really had a way of beating him down, but she picked him right back up again. He wondered if she'd been the same way with Pubes. More importantly, he wondered why she cared about Pubes at all.

"So, where is The Boy Wonderful?"

Will tilted his head. "Ahh, there is still a little sizzle in that stir fry." He waited for a reaction, but she only gave him a cold stare back. "Hey, if he's Boy Wonderful, what does that make me?"

"I don't know. Bat Girl?" She looked at the line of skin care products behind him.

Will shrunk. She already knew more about him than he wished she did. *Hopefully she's good at keeping secrets.* "He doesn't return my calls. He won't text me back."

"He's your friend isn't he?"

Will looked away, rejected. "Used to be…" *Until his penis popularity took over.*

"But not now? What did you do, insult his mother?"

Yes. Many times in fact, but never to her face… "No, no, I wouldn't do that. That might be deadly."

"What about a direct approach? Like, in person?"

Will said nothing. He looked worried. He had tried to contact Pubes many times during the last week, but only by cell phone. He didn't like going over to his house, and he shouldn't have to. Pubes would answer his text messages, if he could. He always did before. *Who knows what I'd discover if I actually went there and knocked on the door...?*

"What, does he live with crazed dogs?"

"Close..."

CHAPTER 14

If she wasn't a girl, *there's no way I'd be standing here right now.* Will hesitated because he knew better, but he rapped lightly on the front door of Pubes's house anyway. He tried to calm himself. His heart was pounding so hard there was simply no stopping it. He knocked again. This was his best friend's place dammit, but a motor pulsating from inside overrode any of those *bosom buddy* thoughts.

Why exactly was there a running motor in there? He knew Leigh was asking herself the same question. He looked at her trying to see through the sidelight. Her persistence to come here had won out over Will's better judgment, but now he was pretty convinced she was having second thoughts. Her face pressed up against the glass showed her curiosity for sure, but the look on that face told Will she would bolt the second someone, or something, looked back at her.

Reluctantly, Will knocked again. Something fired. It wasn't a gun, but it was definitely a shot. That sent Leigh back a few steps, almost landing her into a shrub that lined the garden.

"Eating bush sounds like a better idea than doing this," Will said.

Leigh shuffled to regain her balance. "You wish," she responded nervously. She held a grocery bag in front of her, almost as some type of protection. "Are you luring me into a house with an inescapable basement pit?"

"Good point. I've never been in the basement." Will breathed deeply enough for it to be his last. He really never had been in the basement here. Suddenly, his thoughts about this small Rawlings family became distorted. *Maybe Pubes and his whacko parents are wanted in five states.* "They've never been charged with anything, as far as I know." *Maybe I'm about to become the next national murder story.* "His mother, though… You never can tell with her."

"Comforting. He's expecting you, right?"

"I usually just text him or email, but he's not returning those, remember?" *Maybe he hasn't, because he can't. Maybe his mother…*

"But this time you called…"

Will was ready to cut and run. He was only knocking on this door because of Leigh's convincing eyes, and that just wasn't holding water anymore. She was right—he hadn't called—but it was too late to do anything about that. His plan was to follow her lead. That was simply because he never had a girl so interested in either of them before. Calling wasn't the issue; losing her was, but Will was suddenly reconsidering that whole idea.

"You did call, didn't—"

Another shot fired. *Yes, rethinking this plan is a good thought. Like, right now!* Will turned, ready to rip up the pavement. Unfortunately, his legs didn't move before the door opened.

Norma was there too fast, too close. Instantly, she showed a Lite-Brite smile that Will could almost see his reflection off of. She said something but the motor...

"Turn that—" Norma cleared her throat. "Thing off!" she continued loudly.

Behind Norma, Will saw Ralph looking curiously at a hardwood nailer. He didn't have it placed down on the hardwood the way it should be. It was on its side. Will had no idea how that thing worked, but the way Ralph had it definitely wasn't right. Ralph was inspecting it as if it was jammed. He whacked it with a mallet. A stray nail flew across the room and lodged into the window sill.

Will ducked, but he really had no reason to. Ralph was in another room. Walls protected Will from flying, stray nails. It was just Will's nerves that were shot at that point.

He didn't know if Leigh was still there, and he had no intention of looking to find out. If she was smart, she would be gone. If he'd been smart, he wouldn't be here at all. But now he was stuck. His only chance of getting out of here was to sneak by Norma when she wasn't looking. He watched her intensely for that exact opportunity, but her eyes were pinned on him. He'd seen that look from her before, and he knew she wouldn't back down from greeting her new guests.

The compressor that powered the nailer stopped. Norma was happy again. "Will, come on in." She made the decision easy with an arm wrap that almost turned into a hug. "Hubert will be so, *pumped*." She beamed at the thought of being so cool. "He's been such a grump lately."

The door thud shut. *Shit!* His clear path out of here was suddenly gone with the blink of his eyes. Now he was trapped with an over anxious homemaker and a crazed handyman.

Inside, Will noticed Leigh standing uncomfortably beside him. She was focused on Ralph who examined the nail he'd launched in the nearby living room. At least he wasn't handling the gun anymore, Will thought.

Norma was halfway up the stairs now. This was Will's chance to turn and flee through the *closed door*. Leigh was in the way of the handle, but a small nudge would solve that. *Just get it open and run.* Leigh would follow him. He was sure of that.

"Hubert, Will is here and..." Norma turned back to them with glee. "Who's your girlfriend, Will?"

Will suddenly perked up from that idea. His thoughts

of escaping were instantly gone. The place seemed, *welcoming*. There was no way he could run away from such an encouraging thought. *Pubes's mother... Maybe her curlers aren't that tight after all.*

He turned to Leigh. He was obviously impressed with the concept Norma had just presented. Leigh was not.

"I believe her name's Leigh," Will said while ignoring Leigh's body language.

Norma asked, "And where did you two meet?"

"T-Woks. She speaks fluent Chinese accent."

"Really. I always wanted to speak—" Norma rushed back down, straight to Leigh. "Chinese. Why did you take on such a task, dear?"

Leigh shot a disgusted look at Will.

Will silently celebrated his victory deflection. He didn't expect it, but, man, it felt good to be out of her spotlight.

Leigh hesitated. "Persuasion from an old pseudo Zen Master and Chinese chefs carrying knives," she said.

Norma tilted her head and squinted considering that.

Will's thoughts of security were quickly fading and turning back to being in escape mode. He had the chance he'd been waiting for. He began to slip away until he saw Pubes standing at the top of the stairs. Awesome, Will thought. Leaving would be a better choice, but nothing would happen with Pubes standing there—*right? Surely we can get away from all this unharmed, but only if we move fast.*

The compressor started again. Norma turned away

from Leigh, suddenly enraged. Will rushed for the stairs after he saw Norma pursuing her new challenge.

"Can't you see we have company," he heard her say, but he didn't turn back to see if she was the one throwing nails this time.

He heard another whack; a nail hit something. Will was forced against the railing when Leigh ran past him, desperate for higher ground.

***

Hubert stood in front of his slightly opened bedroom door. He watched Will and Leigh, both struggling to catch their breath. Neither of them dared to move as they listened to Norma and Ralph screaming at each other despite the pulsating compressor.

"Just damn well get used to it," Ralph said.

"I had no intention of going crazy in here."

"You, crazy? Ask our son about that."

There was no response from Norma.

"And you wanted wood. Well, here it is."

Suddenly, the mallet pounded and the nail gun fired, rapid fire. Nails penetrated something. Then there was silence.

Will and Leigh stood there, shocked. Hubert knew what they were thinking, and he was embarrassed. He wasn't all that concerned about his parents, though. The renovations had been getting to both of them, but Hubert had distanced himself from all that. He had other problems. At least when they were plucking away at each other, they kept away from him. The last thing he needed was more of their advice, especially his mother's.

Will said, "Should we check for survivors?"

Hubert slowly turned to the door. He stuck his head into the hallway. He considered going down there to see if everything checked out, but he shut the door instead. The silence was refreshing. Why would he want to disturb that?

"She's fine," Hubert said.

"I don't know," Leigh responded.

"He wouldn't shoot her. He knows better. If he did, trust me, her ghost would come back screaming for blood and broken bones."

"Do you kids want snacks?"

Hubert shook his head and rubbed his eyes, totally embarrassed now. Damn, she was right there at the top of the stairs. He stared at Will and Leigh, trying to figure out what to do.

"Mixed vegetables and a nice light dip maybe?"

"No, Mom."

"How about—"

"No, Mom. Thanks," Hubert said with a little more insistence.

"That dip from last night, Norma? I thought I killed that puppy," Ralph said.

Hubert realized he was staring only at Leigh now. Even as his embarrassment continued—obviously she could tell he was squirming inside—she didn't seem to care. He tried to look away, but it was impossible to ignore her. She was staring back at him; Hubert wasn't sure why. Was she simply terrified into a desperate eye lock, or was she actually interested in him?

"Please, tell me you don't have a dog," Leigh said.

Will asked, "Yeah, man, where's the dog? He's usually all barky, and licky, and happy."

Leigh's knees buckled. She dropped the bag.

Will burst out laughing. "Kidding. Holy shit, you fell for that?"

Thank God for Will, Hubert thought as he blinked the stare away. Only he could save Hubert at a time like this. Why was she here, *in his bedroom*, anyway? The last time he'd seen her—the only time really—he was desperately seeking shelter. How could that insecurity make her want to come here? He went to pick up the bag and spotted a tube of antibiotic ointment on his desk.

Leigh got to the bag first. "I brought my own snacks."

She smiled at him, but Hubert's mind was on his desk. He rushed there and blocked a Post Operation Care Guide that was in open view. "You should have called, Will."

"How many times, Pubes? Next time I'll send up a warning flare. Trust me, this is the last place I want to be without notice."

Hubert was clearly disoriented again, just like in the storage room. This time, however, he was in his own room. "Sorry." Maybe she understood his desperation before, but if he kept this up…

He looked around at his messy room, but he was stuck to the desk because of what he was hiding. "Sorry about the mess. About them." He shot Will a desperate look. "I've been sick."

"No, buddy, not sick…"

Will paused to let Hubert catch up.

Hubert smiled.

"DISEASED!" they both shouted. They laughed which appeared to leave Leigh wondering why.

Will said, "What, you don't think that's funny?" He turned away shaking his head. "Geesh. Where'd you find this chick, Pubes?"

Seriously, Will, I have no idea.

"It's a good thing he did. By the looks of you guys, this fifteen minutes of penis fame is gonna be cut short if I don't step in." She put down the bag and pulled out a brand new T-Woks hat: brim straight and sticker label still on.

"Yeah, you're right," Hubert said.

"Don't get me wrong, without the penis, you're dead before you get off the first shot."

Hubert took a deep breath. He saw Will nearly choke on his. He turned away and saw the care guide again. She had no idea how much that cute, little joke hurt, literally. He shook his head realizing how critical his secret was.

From what Hubert could tell, she wasn't anything like Virginia Almond, but he knew she was only here because of the picture. If he wanted her to go away, all he had to do was expose the secret. But he didn't; he wanted her to stay. So far that picture was nothing but bad news for Hubert, but this wasn't so bad. The picture had put him on her radar, and Hubert was determined to keep it that way.

Hubert suddenly remembered why he was glued to his desk. He couldn't stay like this, so something had to be done. Behind his back, he quickly slid the ointment and the care guide into a drawer.

He kept watching Leigh. He was relieved knowing she didn't catch on. He thought maybe it would be better if the truth did come out, at least to these two. He didn't care so much about Will, but Leigh... "I mean, listen. I wasn't really sick. I—"

He turned away. *No!* She definitely couldn't know about what he'd just gone through. "Yeah, you're right. My time's up. I'm just not—"

"But you can be, and you've got a head start," Leigh said. She took out a pair of hot, big rimmed sunglasses. She handed them to him, but he didn't take them.

"Fuckin' right! He's got a hidden head start," Will added. He laughed; Hubert didn't, and it was like Leigh didn't even hear him.

"It's a bloody penis." Hubert cringed. He didn't need to be doing this to himself. "Big deal." *An extremely big deal.*

"Your penis is the short story here, Hubert. The real story is Virginia Almond," Leigh said.

Will jumped in, "Hey, easy on the size reference. We're talking legend here."

Leigh put on the glasses. "If Virginia wants your penis, all the *Bitches* want your penis."

"And you're the first one in." Will laughed again, solo.

Leigh gave him a cold look, but ignored him otherwise. "If it's what you want, Hubert. Just little changes will put you out there," Leigh continued.

Hubert asked, "Why do you care?" *And why are you here? And after seeing my parents, why are you still here?*

The question appeared to have stumped Leigh. She looked away. Hubert suddenly thought she would come to her senses and hit the road. She looked back at him.

"Why shouldn't I, care? I'm not the type that enjoys watching disasters."

She gave him a look he'd seen from his mother many times. That confused him, and kind of scared him actually.

"I'm more into seeing nature thrive." She pulled a cucumber from the bag. "It's a natural thing." She smiled with raised eyebrows.

He sighed with relief. She instantly came back to being Leigh, not a teenaged version of his mother.

Next, she pulled out two small avocados. Hubert had no idea where this was going, but he was beginning to think the whole maintenance crew would burst through the door. All of them in on a huge joke.

"We start with getting you a complexion like Will who has no clue how to get it without Proactiv or Retin-A." She also took out some yogurt and a jar of honey. She crumpled up the empty bag.

Hubert went back to his door and looked into the hallway. *Yep, something's definitely up, and my crazy parents are probably in on it too.*

Will said, "With that?"

There was nothing suspicious out there. Hubert turned back to his room. It didn't look like anything else was going on. He saw Will check himself out in the mirror.

"Retin-A is only part of this sweet complexion cocktail," Will said to himself.

"Works for Chester. It should for you too," Leigh said.

Will looked confused. "Chester..."

"He's just looking for the same thing you are, Will. You know, you're all the same." She looked directly at Hubert.

Will asked, "If you're in so tight with Chester, why aren't you with all the, *Bitches*, instead of here with no one?"

She stayed focused on Hubert. "Not all girls think alike, Will. That's the way it should be." She gave Hubert that question mark smile again.

"Listen, I just haven't got anything to offer." Hubert turned away and looked out the window. "Any more..."

"But I can change that."

Hubert looked back as she was scanning the desk.

"I need a bowl. You'll see." She forced eye-to-eye contact.

Hubert panicked slightly. *What's going to happen to me now?* He desperately tried to keep this confusion to himself.

"Will, go get a bowl," she said.

Will turned sharply. "What? Are you fucking insane? They're conducting hardwood warfare down there."

Absolutely, Will, and there's no way you're leaving me up here alone with... Hubert moved quickly for the door. "He's right. I'll get it."

Will suddenly countered to block Hubert's escape. "No! I got it." He got to the door first. "Hardwood support," he said quietly to Hubert. "Bowl, rhymes with—" He shot Hubert a laser stare.

"I don't know where the bowl is," Hubert said desperately to Will. He turned to Leigh, worried. "With the renovation and all."

"Seriously, didn't you read the instructions?" Will opened the door a crack. He looked but didn't go out. He turned back.

Hubert knew Will could tell he was scared shitless. He hoped his parents had done the same to Will. The second

Will said anything about going down there again, Hubert would be out of here in a flash.

"Christ, man. Just open up the cupboard, mess around a little, and you'll find the hole—I mean bowl." Will looked back to the door.

***

Reluctantly, Will stepped into the hallway. Going down there, with shots firing, was way more than he envisioned doing during this visit, but what Pubes was about to experience far exceeded his expectations too. He simply had no choice. He had to put up this sacrifice for the greater good.

Things seemed to have calmed down between Norma and Ralph anyway. They had probably made up by now and were carrying on doing whatever weird people their age do. Will just had to stay unnoticed. If they saw him, he had no idea what would happen to him. If he saw them... He shuddered at the thought of what was involved when Norma and Ralph *made up*.

He took a cautious step. He heard Leigh say, "Will, a knife and spoon too." He rolled his eyes as he slowly approached the stairs. The knife wasn't a bad idea, though. A warrior in the battlefield required a weapon. Will in Hubert's kitchen... He wanted more, but a knife would have to do. He'd go for that first.

Will listened at the top of the stairway: silence. He started down.

***

Hubert still stood at the door, unable to move. With Leigh in front of him, he felt trapped. It would be nothing for him to go to his desk or sit on his bed, but being close to the door was probably best. There, he at least had a chance to get away if he had to.

"Is he always going to be such a large obstacle?"

Hubert looked back to the hallway. "Will can find ways to be invisible. He just doesn't want to miss anything." *And I wish he were here right now so nothing will happen for him to miss.*

Leigh softened. "You need to be as determined as he is."

"Determined, fearless... Desperate?"

"Desperate to get what he doesn't have? That's not necessarily a bad thing."

She was right, and he knew it. The only problem was, Hubert wasn't desperate to have the same things Will wanted. At least not the way all of this was happening. If nothing else, it was just too fast for Hubert to handle. Too many clinging girls; too many hunky dudes; too many well-wishers in his bedroom.

He wasn't even sure what Leigh's intentions were, but

he couldn't help feel he had a hidden target in his pants, and there was a contest going on for someone to claim victory. He hadn't been at the food court for a week now, and he had no idea who had entered that race. *Of course, only I know differently—about the target that is.*

***

Will had snuck slowly down the stairs. At the bottom, he saw Ralph examining the row of nail damage on his living room wall. Will slid slowly against the wall. No sudden noises or crazy surprises, he thought without taking his eyes off Ralph. He slipped by without Ralph noticing.

Ahead of Will was the treacherous landscape of a heavily furnished kitchen. He climbed in with a cupboard as his target destination. Fuck me, he thought while straddling the arm of a sofa. *Who other than the Rawlings would have their kitchen set up for lounging?*

Will made it through. He reached for the door handle. He pulled on the door.

"Ralph, choose between all meat with a smoldering hot sauce or small, savory courses of temptation," Will heard Norma say.

He panicked not knowing where she was. He was wide open if she came in here: a prowler in the pantry. He grabbed a bowl, and it slipped from his hands. He fumbled it on its way to the ground and saved it from disaster. He heard footsteps on the stairs from the basement. He spun around: furniture.

He started to navigate through it. The footsteps got louder: closer.

"Ralph, I need to know what I'm making for dinner because once I'm in the kitchen, knives start flyin'," Norma said.

Will stopped suddenly. He turned back, pulled open a drawer, and snap up a knife and spoon.

"Jesus, Norma…," Ralph said.

The compressor started. Will bolted for the hallway.

"As long as it's hot, any ol' shit will do," Ralph yelled over the compressor's noise.

***

Norma entered the kitchen. She was confused. She felt like something had just moved in here, but more importantly… "What did you just say?"

Despite the compressor, she had heard Ralph. She knew what he said, and it wasn't leaving a favorable impression. Her temper slowly boiled over.

***

Hubert was shocked when Will rushed into his

bedroom. Hubert had moved away from the door. He was now sitting on his bed while Leigh worked at his desk with the stuff she'd brought. He just started to get to an acceptable comfort level with Leigh, but Will would surely change that.

Will leaned against the closed door, panting for each breath. "Mission accomplished?"

Hubert looked away. No smile or acknowledgment communicated clearly that nothing went down here. Will was staring at him, but at least Will had the decency not to blast him in front of Leigh. Will must have known nothing would happen between him and Leigh anyway. Thinking otherwise would be just his mind working overtime.

Finally, Will moved. Hubert watched him hand over the bowl and cutlery to Leigh. The silence was nerve wracking. Just a short time ago, Hubert was all alone here and everything was fine… Well, not really.

When these two had first come here, Hubert wasn't ready for Will and definitely not Leigh or the food court. He was happy to see them, though. They gave him time away from the renovation nightmare, and from his mother's consistent post operation maintenance reminders. But Will was just as annoying in many ways, and bringing Leigh here wasn't making things any better. He saw Will look back at him, totally disappointed, like a father scorning his loser son.

Hubert tried to ignore him. Will wasn't going anywhere,

but he wasn't talking. At least Hubert could cling to that while it lasted.

He watched Leigh go to work with the things she'd brought. These two had plans that definitely revolved around him. If he was going to stop it, it would have to be now. For some reason, however, he couldn't do that—he didn't want to.

He saw the new hat Leigh had brought lying beside him. He picked it up and checked it out before putting it on. He tilted it a bit to the side. It looked better that way. The glasses were there too. He went to grab them, but Leigh spun around from the desk while checking the consistency of what she had mixed up in the bowl.

Will watched her, still saying nothing. He seemed to know what she was working on, but Hubert didn't have a clue. Will was mesmerized by it. Leigh put the bowl down on the desk, right in front of Will.

Hubert got up and checked himself out in a full-length mirror with the new hat on. He saw Leigh looking at him in the mirror too. She gave him a look of approval. A new hat; nicer shades. What harm could that do, he thought? Leigh was suddenly right behind him and still impressed. He smiled at her in the mirror.

She smiled back and playfully tried to get him to wear his pants lower. He desperately tried to stop her, both of them laughing during the wrestling match.

Hubert turned away from her to see Will with his hair

slicked back and looking great. If he didn't know what Leigh had created, he certainly found a use for it. He licked his fingers after putting down the jar of honey.

***

Hubert walked awkwardly with Will along the upstairs hallway. The crotch of their pants hung at their knees. Leigh was right with them, coaching every movement. It was a good thing she was too. Wearing pants like this took some getting used to. Hubert definitely needed her direction to get him through it.

This was what Hubert liked so much about being friends with Will. His adventures were sometimes too much, but without him, Hubert would be lost. Now, Leigh seemed to be fitting right in with their goofiness. It was a good feeling for Hubert after everything he'd been through. Before they came, he was just about as low as he could be. They changed that.

He reached the end of the hallway. They turned, both of them nearly falling. Hubert saw their reflection in a wall mirror at the end of the hall. The three of them broke up at the sight of their faces plastered with a cucumber-avocado mask.

***

Hubert sat with Will on the edge of Hubert's bed. The masks were washed off, but Leigh still worked her creations like she was born to accessorize.

She'd obviously come here with a purpose, Hubert thought. She stood them up and fussed with their hair; she adjusted their clothes. She worked on both of them as though they were one. She had it all rolling just the way she wanted, and it looked like nothing would stop her now.

Leigh stood behind them. Hubert examined himself in the mirror with Will right beside him. Leigh nodded her approval from behind. Even the food court wasn't ready for this. Hubert felt like he was looking at two completely different guys. They were no longer losers like everyone knew them as. They were cool; they had swagger. They looked like born again rap stars.

***

Hubert pulled a T-shirt over his head. He was dressed back in his comfort zone. The fame costume Leigh had created was neatly folded on his desk. It had been fun when Will and Leigh were here, but he looked at it now like the clothes might bite if he got too close.

The person he really was would be hidden behind all those clothes if he chose to put them on and take on the food court again. He wasn't sure if he could play that role.

He already had to some extent, but this would be taking it full scale.

That, and the secret he had in his pants, was so overwhelming. The guy doing that wasn't him, but he doubted anyone at the food court was really who they appeared to be. Maybe this had been his problem all along. Maybe he should dump Hubert Rawlings, and *Pubes* should show up for his next appearance.

"Hubert, come down for dinner, sweetheart. You won't want to miss out on this one," his mother said.

Hubert nodded. The reality of where he was now, and his mother's dominance here, practically slapped him in the face. He turned away from his desk and headed out of his bedroom.

Hubert stopped at the entrance of the kitchen. He'd just been through a great time with Will and Leigh. It had started off terrifying but ended up awesome. Now he had to survive dinner with his parents, in a living room kitchen no less.

He stayed at the entrance and watched his mother put finishing touches on a prepared dinner plate. He thought about just grabbing it and leaving. She might not even notice considering the chaos going on down here. She turned, excited to see him.

"Careful, dear. There could be knives." She looked throughout the furniture and cracked a smile. "I wouldn't want to see you get cut."

Hubert shot her a look. No doubt she just thought she was being funny, but really...

She took the prepared plate and started on an obstacle course to put it on the table. "Ralph, it's getting cold."

His father showed up at the doorway wearing a day's worth of sawdust. "Whatever it is we're eatin', it's gotta taste better than these wooden teeth." He smiled while licking his teeth.

Hubert shook his head confirming how desperate he was to grab the food and run.

His mother put down a beautiful dinner in front of Hubert.

His father plopped himself down in his assigned place.

Hubert was still reluctant to sit down, but he didn't see that he had a choice. He watched his mother turn back to the counter. She turned on the microwave.

"Heat it up a little for my hubby." She looked back to both of them. Her smile seem odd to Hubert. She popped the microwave door. "Keep licking your lips, dear. That'll be your dessert first..."

Both Hubert and his father winced as his mother spun around with his father's plate.

"After a full course of any ol' shit." She plopped a plate full of garnished shit in front of his father.

The room was completely silent, followed by his father's jaw that nearly hit the table. Hubert looked away not fully understanding who the seventeen-year-old was here.

His father took his fork. He poked it a little. "Wow, this baby's freshly baked."

Hubert slowly slipped away. "Oh, man. And these are my pillars of advice," he said to himself.

His mother asked, "What's that, dear?"

He ignored her.

CHAPTER 15

While he stood at the checkout counter under an *Only Donut Holes* sign, Danny finished up with a customer after selling her a box of donut holes. He plucked a hole from a display tray. He held it with a disgusted finger pinch. "Rand, your hole is too big."

"Well, you made it that way," Rand said from the back room.

Danny shook his head slightly, trying to ignore Rand's twisted sense of humor. "Just a quick position change on the machine will solve this problem. You know that."

Rand stuck his head through the serving counter. "Trust me, sweetheart, when you set the machine, we're gonna get a big hole."

Danny turned away, frustrated. The look on his face sent Rand a clear message: Danny wasn't feeling *frisky* today.

"Anyway, customers like it that way," Rand continued.

"Forget the customers." Danny held up the donut hole. "How are we going to survive with a hole this big?"

Rand came out from the back. "Geesh, Danny. What's with all the fuss?"

Danny wasn't exactly sure what Rand was referring to because a commotion had started up in the eating section of the food court. He looked at Rand, but Rand wasn't looking at him. Danny turned back to the commotion.

From the distance, two dudes approached the food court as though they had stage lights following them. Their swagger and accessories put a temporary stop to hunger.

"It's a different taste everyone's lookin' for, Danny. Size is just an option," Rand said.

Danny saw that Rand was still watching what everyone else was. Rand took the donut hole that Danny was holding, but he didn't take his eyes off the attraction.

"Personally, I like mine glazed." Rand popped the hole in his mouth and turned to Danny with a sensual look.

Danny looked away. Sometimes it was impossible to figure out what went on in Rand's mind. Strangely, though, Danny liked him that way.

One of the superstars slid by the counter, close enough for Danny to touch, and close enough for him to notice it was the guy who had been in the back room—the guy in the picture.

"And together with him, you're sportin' the same flavor," Rand said from behind Danny.

The guy from the picture heard that and turned to both of them. He kept moving, but Danny noticed his stride suffer a little.

The picture had stuck with Danny, and it appeared that Rand hadn't forgotten about it either. It seemed odd that a shy kid, in that extremely awkward situation, would leave such an impression on the two of them and everyone else here. It's an offbeat fascination he figured.

Danny looked back at Rand who was giving him a look of approval. A smile spread over Rand's face.

Rand swallowed the hole and licked his fingers. "But since we're talkin' about donut holes..." He licked his lips.

Danny turned away and watched the two celebrities make their way into the eating section.

***

Leigh scooped rice onto a serving plate, but she was preoccupied with something beyond her customer, who happened to be Chester.

She knew this moment would come today, and she had been anxious about it ever since she started her shift. She wasn't sure how everyone at the food court would react, and she didn't know if Hubert—or Will for that matter—could pull it off. The last time she'd seen them, they seemed up for the challenge, though. Only time would tell if they would soar to greater heights or fall flat on their faces.

Chester held up his hands in disbelief. "Easy, easy. You know the drill."

Finally, she acknowledged Chester was there but just barely. He watched closely as Leigh filled his order out of habit.

"You didn't call," Chester said.

Leigh ignored him, but she continued to complete his plate with a scoop of red sauce on the rice. She looked back at Hubert and Will working the food court. Actually, they did little more than walk through the sitting area. She had never thought they were capable of more than that, so her work with them was paramount to their success.

"Ah, ah. A little more," Chester said making sure she got his fried rice right.

She obliged Chester instinctively and noticed everyone watching Hubert and Will. Even the Bitches found the performance entertaining enough for them to turn their attention away from themselves.

So far they were doing great, and they actually seemed to be enjoying themselves. She expected that from Will, but Hubert was the unknown here. Based on what she'd seen from him before, the tables could turn any moment.

"There, perfect."

Leigh flung Chester's plate onto the counter.

"Well, we gonna do this or what?"

After a second of dead air, she realized Chester had just asked her a question. It took her a bit to figure out what he was talking about. She shook her head to clear the haze. "Yeah, sure, Chester. Timings off a little right now, but right, we will."

Her answer was simply intended to satisfy his question. She really wanted him to move along and stop obstructing her view. Things could get nasty out there for Hubert. She needed to be able to react if it did, and having Chester in her face would only prevent her from doing that.

She tried to focus back on Hubert, but she noticed another customer push a take-out carton to Tung at the cash register.

"I ordered Szechuan Noodles, but there's rice in here," the customer said.

Tung hesitated. He had a harsh look for Leigh.

Leigh snapped out of her trance again. *Shit. The last thing I need now is having to figure out what this hyper Chinese Shih Tzu Man is yelling at me.* She snatched the carton just before Tung was about to take it.

"Sorry about that," she said to the confused customer. She flung the carton into the garbage and started filling another with noodles.

She watched Tung growl as he rung Chester through.

***

Will led the way, and he could see Pubes beside him working all the moves they'd been taught. Will was ready for this, more than he could have ever imagined. He hadn't expected Leigh to come up with this makeover, but she simply had a magic touch. It felt great to be wrapped up in the package she created. He was pretty much floating now that everything was going just the way he'd always envisioned.

He made his way deeper into the food court knowing Pubes was riding the same wave, right along with him. Will saw Leigh watching them from the distance. He gave Pubes a directional tap without missing a single cool step. Best to stay close to their maker, he thought. She had got them this far, and she appeared ready to launch them into stardom.

They approached the T-Woks counter. Just as Will was about to open his mouth, a tray crashed next door at Mexican Heaven. Javier wailed, mourning the loss of more tacos. He continued with rapid fire Spanish ranting. Will looked annoyed by the distraction. He tried again.

"Slide me noodle, an e-roll and some bird, lemon coated." He said that with less confidence than he'd planned. The interruption put him off a bit, but he quickly recomposed himself and delivered the line. It came out a little shaky; he knew that. It was a good thing Leigh was looking back at him.

Leigh raised her eyebrows. She laughed.

***

She looked at Hubert standing next to Will. Leigh was impressed. He looked great, but better than that, he was rockin' the new *Pubes* she had put together.

"Okay, Will. A cookie with that?"

"Baby, I got a cookie in my trousers that needs serving."

Leigh was not paying any attention to Will. Instead, she gave Hubert a look over. She actually found it amazing that he'd taken it this far. Judging by the Hubert she knew before, she was doubtful the *Pubes* she created would emerge. But he seemed to be doing fine. All he needed to do now was stay calm and let things roll on, just the way they should.

"And there ain't no cookie worth eatin' after a plate of Will," Will continued.

The fact that Will was still talking broke her attention away from Hubert. She watched the line from Mexican Heaven begin to fill up behind them. Leigh had Will's plate under construction. She saw Will notice the line. He turned for a performance. She cringed at the thought of what he might do.

Leigh signaled for Tung. "The hats."

She was still scouting Hubert also. She knew he liked

her watching him. She thought the line would panic him, but it was like he didn't even know it was there.

Will, on the other hand, seemed ready for anything.

"Just hold my cookie, sweetheart. It looks like I'm about to have my hands full," Will said.

Suddenly, Leigh thought that Hubert may not realize anything else was going on around him. He seemed mesmerized with her. She tried to break his focus on her. She motioned for him to turn around.

Just then, Virginia appeared and rubbed up against Hubert. She wrapped her hands around his waist, then lower.

Damn, Leigh thought.

Hubert instantly lost all his cool and instinctively covered up. This was just what Leigh had worried about. She doubted he would be able to handle Virginia Almond, but she didn't think he would have to deal with her, at least not this quickly. She could tell Hubert was desperately losing it. She knew this would happen if it all turned against him. She panicked not knowing what to do with the counter in the way.

Virginia licked Hubert's ear, slightly. He tightened his grip. Virginia said, "I doubt there's anything here to satisfy a guy as delicious as you. Care for something else to eat?"

Virginia did nothing to keep that message quiet. It was as though Leigh was part of the conversation. Leigh said back to her in the bad Chinese accent, "Your order, Sir?"

Leigh smiled while Hubert looked up desperately at her. He needed a distraction, but she doubted her comment would be enough. She had a crowd in front of her, and they were the answer but how...?

She saw the hats Tung had placed on the counter. She wrapped her arm around all of them and pulled them close to the cash register.

Leigh pointed to the T-Walks hat Hubert was wearing with her eyes bulging at the guys closest to her. There was a brief second while guys in the line noticed the attention Hubert was getting from Virginia. Then, they surged for hats.

Virginia was knocked away from Hubert and face-to-face with Will. Leigh watched Will hesitate with a reaction, but he was quick with his recovery. He created a distraction for Hubert, and Leigh noticed Hubert slip away.

Virginia gave Leigh a bitch look.

Leigh asked again, "Your order, Sir?"

Chester took up a spot behind Virginia leaving Will standing there alone again. Chester pulled the same move Virginia had done on Hubert.

Virginia looked at Chester and Will beside him. She turned to Leigh then bolted.

Chester stood there staring at Leigh. She grinned, victorious. "You need a hat," she said to Chester in her bad Chinese accent.

CHAPTER 16

Only minutes ago, Will was cool and confident. In a flash, the mob was gone, the spotlight was off, and Pubes was nowhere to be seen. Will was alone again, which was something he had been extremely used to, but he expected more now. He felt like he'd jumped that hurdle and busted through the elusive doors that had held him back for so long.

Without Pubes by his side, however, he was nothing, and he knew it. But Will wasn't the type who would sit around and feel sorry for himself. He had felt it all within his grasp, and he definitely knew how to get that ticket back. He just didn't know where that back stage pass was now, so he searched. He looked through the table section and in the vendor lines. Pubes was gone.

He couldn't have gotten too far, but the food court was packed; T-Woks hats were everywhere. The last time

Pubes had panicked in this type of situation, Will remembered him jumping the counter. That, and the fact that Pubes worked here now, quickly made Will realize that Pubes would know how to get out of here, fast. Will was probably stuck to finding Pubes at that dreaded last resort: his house.

Will almost gave up, then he saw him, at least he thought it was him. The guy Will saw didn't have a T-Woks hat on, but Will knew the clothes... He looked down at what he was wearing. No one else had on clothes like this, and he suddenly felt uncomfortable being the only one. He beelined toward the washrooms.

Will stopped just before Pubes was about to open the side door. "What the hell, Pubes? You've got a social responsibility here."

***

Hubert didn't look back. He was surprised he'd gotten this far without Will finding him, but the inevitable confrontation would have to happen sooner or later. It might as well be now. "Go ahead, Will. I'm done with it."

When Hubert had left the whole situation at T-Woks, he was certain he had to get out of there. He'd thought he could make this image change work, but as soon as Virginia entered the picture, all bets were off.

His focus had been to get the hat and shades off, get

out of these clothes, and get as far away from the food court as he could.

He knew Will would be chasing him. Now that he'd caught up, Hubert kind of wanted to keep the gig going, but he couldn't. Sure, Will would always be there with him, but all the attention would be on Hubert. He would be the one who would have to perform. Emotionally, he just wasn't ready for that. Physically, he was not the same person. In fact, he was a fraud, and Virginia Almond would take no time to expose that if he let it all happen.

"What? What do ya mean, done with it? We just got started," Will continued.

Hubert turned, defeated, like a melting Slurpee. "You take it from here. I'm just not up to it." He opened the door. All he had to do was walk away. If Will followed, fine. Hubert kinda wished he would and it would be all over.

"Jesus, man. At least wait and see what happens."

Hubert snapped back. "And that's exactly what I'm afraid of, Will. I know what's gonna happen." He shook his head and turned away.

"Lead with your dick, man. What the hell's wrong with you?"

Will was right. Hubert struggled with the fact that any other seventeen-year-old would jump all over this. No one would care about the circumcision. It was healed; he was ready to go, but he wasn't like that. "I'd tell you, Will, but there's no point. You're good to go without me."

"No, Pubes, you're wrong. I'm only any good with you. Don't you get that?"

"Guess I don't, and really, I shouldn't have to."

Hubert took one last look at Will. He was hoping to get something from him: some compassion; some understanding. But Will wasn't capable of anything like that, especially at a time like this.

Instead of continuing to explain himself, or actually coming out with the secret, Hubert opened the door wider and left.

***

Will approached the counter at T-Woks. He still had his T-Woks hat on, and the clothes did wonders to light him up; but without the moves, he just seemed out of place. He wasn't concerned about that now, however. He needed to get Pubes back into the ring. After just seeing him, he didn't know if that was possible, even with Leigh's help.

He saw Leigh busy with customers, but he knew she was dying to know where Pubes was. He didn't want to have to explain what he didn't understand himself, though. He thought about just moving along and putting this all behind him. She'd done all she could. If Pubes couldn't come through with what he needed to do, what more could Will expect from her?

Leigh gave him a *what's up* look. That stopped Will from walking away. He didn't know what to tell her, but she was finishing up with a customer. Maybe she could do something...

Will shook his head when Leigh was right in front of him. He looked down at all the Chinese food. "He ate the last *Egg Roll*. Gave a new meaning to *Chicken Balls*." Will took off his hat. He looked at it and all the others floating around in the food court. "He put away his *Wong Tong* for, no reason." Will buried his shaking head.

"Where'd he go?"

CHAPTER 17

Hubert opened the locker room door and stepped into the hallway holding his T-Woks hat. Rod was behind him.

When Hubert came to the food court today, he wasn't scheduled for a shift. He had no idea if Rod would even be here when he rushed to the locker room. Fortunately, Rod was there, and he was alone.

Another fortunate thing for Hubert was that Rod seemed to understand the anxiety Hubert was going through. Hubert didn't have to say much at all. Rod knew what Hubert would say before he even opened his mouth. It was as though Rod expected it.

"You're sure, Hubert? You can think about it if you want."

"No, Rod, thanks. I just don't have what everyone thinks I've got."

Hubert started to walk away, satisfied with how

smoothly that talk went. Rod thought Hubert was trying too hard to fit in. How couldn't he with the way Hubert looked. Rod also knew Hubert wasn't a match with the rest of the crew, so he left it open. The decision was Hubert's, and he made it.

With this job out of the way, all Hubert would have to do now is ditch the clothes and get himself back the way he'd always been. His only problem was Will. He needed Will. Without him, the only people in Hubert's life would be his parents. He shook his head not sure what he would do.

Right away, he could sense someone else was down here with him. He started to panic thinking the worst: Virginia. A chill rushed through his body: head to toe. He heard Leigh's voice instead.

"What is it, exactly, that you feel you're missing?"

Hubert closed his eyes and sighed. He had done fine getting away from Will's persistence, and Rod's obstacle of getting out of the maintenance crew job had not been a problem at all. But Leigh would be a different story. He reluctantly looked up. Leigh was blocking his way.

"Is there something you're hiding that we haven't already seen? Some special part that doesn't work the way it should?" She cracked a smile, obviously hoping for a light moment. "Some defect in the Pubes Machine?"

What the hell do you know? Please don't tell me you've been talking to my mother. "You have no idea."

"No, I think I do." She stepped forward. She was suddenly serious. "It's just that the hole you want to crawl back into isn't big enough for two."

She stopped with no more than an arm's reach between them. She couldn't have been clearer. *If I go, everything I like about this girl goes right out the door too.* Again, the decision was his.

"You know, you don't have to take it so seriously," she said.

She was saying the same as Rod had said. Why was he the only one who didn't think this way? "Easy for you to say. You're just coaching from the sidelines."

"But I'm playing the same game you are, just against a different set of players."

She looked away, like she was considering her situation and what she should reveal.

"They all want to score, Hubert. I just don't let them. It's that simple." She stared him down. "It can be the same set of rules for you."

She took his hat and straightened it out. He watched her playing with the hat and realized what she just said made sense. He was always so quick to panic every time things got rough. Instead, he just needed to calm down and stand his ground if it came to that.

"When someone comes around with their made up game face on, you get to decide if they win or not. It may be tougher for guys to do that, but there's no rule saying you can't." She put on the hat like she owned it. "And no one's saying you don't get to play at all."

But as soon as it gets anywhere close to a goal, something inside me blows one nasty whistle, and the game's over before it even started.

She tilted the hat. "But only the players get any action." She smiled.

Wow. Hubert doubted that anyone would ever see him as any type of *player*, but he certainly got her point.

"If you crawl back into your hole… She looked beyond Hubert. She shrugged. "I guess the game's over."

He shook his head trying to clear up his understanding that there was actually a girl, standing right here, wanting him to be himself. She'd dressed him up to fit in; she exploited his situation to capitalize; but really, he was a lot like her. He just needed a better act.

So it's decision time, Hubert Pubes Rawlings. He looked back to the locker door where Leigh was looking.

Rod still stood there.

CHAPTER 18

Sleeping on it, with a huge smile on his face, made a world of difference. If Virginia derailed Hubert yesterday, Leigh put him right back on track with a plan that suddenly made more sense than anything Will had ever came up with.

With extreme confidence, Hubert strode down the hallway toward the locker room door. Yesterday he was leaving here for good, but now he had this. His T-Woks hat was in place, and he was dressed to deliver nothing but cool.

Hubert burst in. A wall of jocks, all focused on the door, stopped him dead. His spirit shriveled. His knees buckled from the sheer blaze of all those pissed off eyes.

Chester was up front and center. At first he said nothing. No one did. The silence put Hubert even more on edge, creating a room with the tension of bending glass.

Hubert didn't have a clue what the problem was. The only thing he'd done was change a bit so he would fit in better. He thought the *Hubert* from the past had been an eye sore for these guys; the *Pubes* he was now worked well with the image of this maintenance crew. In fact, Leigh had probably planned it that way, so what could possibly be wrong?

Then he remembered the looks he'd been getting from these guys. The food court attention had shifted to him which had always been theirs. He hadn't taken any of that seriously, but he realized now how much of a mistake that was. He could tell by their determination and intensity, that they weren't about to let a little shit like Hubert *Pubes* Rawlings take this any further.

Chester smiled without really meaning it. He turned away shaking his head. "Did you really think you were going to single-handedly take what's rightfully ours?"

Damn! Wasn't there at least a chance I was wrong? Hubert shook his head not sure how to react. Popularity came with being part of this group. *Now they think I want it all to myself?* But that couldn't have been further from the truth. All Hubert really wanted was Leigh. Even she was a stretch, but she put him out here. She was the only reason he came back.

Chester turned sharply, almost ready to bite. "With that?" Chester swatted the brim of Hubert's T-Woks hat.

It tumbled to the floor. He looked Hubert up and down.

Where was Will now, Hubert thought? It was times like this when Hubert needed Will's guaranteed distraction the most. Or Leigh for that matter... If she were here, this whole situation would be nonexistent. But Hubert couldn't go around having to rely on them to rescue him. If he was going to play this image thing out, he would have to stand up for himself.

Chester backed off. He took a much needed breath, for both himself and Hubert. "I can't believe all this has even happened. Frankly, Pubes, I need to see for myself." He stepped back to include the human wall behind him. "We all need proof."

So how do I quickly deal with these guys struggling over how they've lost everything because of—oh shit! The picture... Hubert instinctively covered his crotch with both hands and crossed legs.

With everything that had happened since that eventful first meeting with these guys, Hubert had forgotten about the picture. They probably all had it on their cell phones. They've probably studied it and tried to figure out how to make it work in their favor. But to them, Hubert had something they didn't. It was something they could never have. Everything was slipping away from them because of it, and now they had to act.

What would they do with Hubert standing right in front of them? They could only see for themselves what was killing their action. If they did that, what could Hubert do about it? He looked around frantically for an escape route. He was trapped—doomed when his secret gets out.

Chester moved first then all the others. If it wasn't for his mother, Hubert could simply pull down his pants to avoid this imminent mobbing. That was no longer an option, though. Running, again, seemed like Hubert's only way out, but he had nowhere to go.

They all stepped closer then T-Woks hats appeared. Chester put his on. He gestured to Hubert for his approval. "Tilted right or left? Which is better?"

CHAPTER 19

Will waited patiently for his order at Mark Saint John's Fried Burgers when the crew moved into the food court with a flurry of teamwork. The excitement not only got Will's attention but everyone else's too. Their uniforms were coordinated and each guy wore a T-Woks hat. They were fast-paced and synchronized, like a scripted dance crew of a pop star.

Of course, the show centered on the new star of this food court. Pubes had none of the abilities his crewmates did, but at this point he didn't need talent. He just needed to be there. By the looks of it, he didn't need Will either.

Will shook his head in disbelief, but he couldn't help being impressed by the performance. Unfortunately, he was left out. He looked around at everyone watching. Somehow, he needed to be part of this sweet action.

He saw Tung watching them from behind his cash

register at T-Woks. He could tell this was a proud moment for Tung. T-Woks hats were everywhere. It was like Tung had set up a promotional gig with top-notch choreography. He smiled and swayed to the crews movements while he rung in another hat sale.

Close by at Mexican Heaven, Javier tried to offload a stack of taco shells, but he got distracted by Tony and Drew performing an entertaining act of mop-and-dry. Will cringed, knowing what was about to happen with Javier involved. The tacos started to teeter. Javier tried desperately for a recovery, but tacos crashed in front of his counter.

Instantly, Javier's inventory was gone, but Tony and Drew didn't miss a beat. They slid past Will for immediate clean up action. Will started to join them, but his first step couldn't keep up. The next few put him back waiting for his burger order.

Will's burger was nowhere in sight, but the vendors gave him solid entertainment during the wait. Abid from Sub Attack was quick to get out from behind his counter with a tray of samples for Javier's dismayed customers. Will looked to see how his burger was doing. There was little progress, so he stepped away and grabbed a few samples before Abid got away.

Rocco tried the genuine appeal of Italian persuasion. "Slices right here, straight from my grandfather's hot ovens," he said with a heavy Italian accent.

Will found himself caught in the middle when Abid spun around. "Grandfather's ovens? Try cleaning them, Rocco, so we can see last year's install date," he replied in Pakistani like English. Abid pressed on with more samples which left Rocco steaming and allowed Will to snag a few more.

Despite being thoroughly captivated, Will was still waiting. He looked up at the partially burnt out Mark Saint John's Fried Burgers sign. The sign actually read: *Mark aint   Fried   .*

Will turned back to the food court. He desperately wanted to try his cool act, but he couldn't upstage what he was watching. Instead, he stayed at the counter listening to the background arguing of Mark struggling with his tuned-out teenaged staff.

***

Hubert, on the other hand, worked magic with his cleaning gig in the table section. With hardly any effort required, his female response was extraordinary. Girls watched him but kept their distance. They tried to lure him with sexy poses and eye contact. Hubert just stuck to his game plan, though. He was out there in the field, but the popular custodian was on a different level now.

He'd been doing fine when it was just Will and him, but now the whole crew had his back. If he got himself in too deep, the crew would be there. The Virginia's of the food court would have to deal with them. That's exactly what Will wanted his role to be, but he simply didn't have what it would take to control this madness.

Hubert saw Leigh sitting with two girls, obviously taking up a table for observation only. They were heavy into a conversation that seemed focused on the activity here. That was mostly centered on Hubert, so these girls were likely talking about him.

One of the girls shot off a disgusted look, but it kind of looked like she was jealous. They continued their conversation with their heads swinging from the maintenance crew, to the Bitches, and back to each other.

Suddenly, Leigh caught Hubert's eye. That stopped the conversation. The other two were looking at him. Everyone was, but it didn't bother him. As long as he had space, Hubert was working with this just fine.

He headed their way. The two with Leigh suddenly seemed stressed. They straightened up as he approached. Hubert sat down right beside Leigh. He took an exhausting breath. "Whew. A lot of messes out there today. I'm not sure I can keep it up."

He smiled at Leigh, then at the others. They were mesmerized. They said nothing.

"My friends. Elle, Jane," Leigh said.

There was nothing from either of them: silence, at a table for four.

"They're usually more opinionated than this." Leigh flipped them a look.

"Well, the table's clean, and there's nothing to spill." Hubert started to get up.

"No, go ahead, clean it," Jane said. She smiled self-consciously at Elle and Leigh. "That'd be nice. Right?"

Hubert jumped right into action.

"And speaking about clean, you really should think about getting some work done on…" Jane hesitated. "Well, you know." She paused again. "It."

Hubert abruptly stopped cleaning. *What did she just say?* If Hubert wasn't looking right at her, he would have sworn she was his mother. He'd spent his entire life listening to continuous reminders about cleaning his penis. He figured the operation would at least save him from never having to hear penis cleaning warnings again.

He buried his head and rushed the cleaning job. His confidence was suddenly gone like the power just went out. That rush of anxiety washed over him. He looked around quickly, feeling like everything was closing in.

He saw Leigh shoot Jane a stare.

He noticed Elle was shocked by the comment too.

"Well, it can't be a healthy thing being like that," Jane continued.

Hubert finished up but not very well.

"Christ, Jane, go ahead, ask him about his hygienic routine for uncircumcised penis care," Elle said.

That set Hubert back a few steps too. Holy shit, he thought. These two have no filter whatsoever. And they're Leigh's friends... How could she be hanging out with them? She wasn't like that, at least not the Leigh he knew. She had been instrumental in him getting to this point. He trusted her, almost more than he trusted Will. No, definitely more than Will. If there was anyone he would tell about his circumcision, it would be Leigh. But if he did, would she tell these two?

If Will found out he would probably keep it quiet because he would have too much to lose with that secret out there. If Leigh knew, she would support him, at least he thought she would. If these two came upon that juicy piece of information... *Man, I gotta get out of this place.*

Jane jumped in with a shaky defense. "Hey, it's on public display. Should be fair game for conversation too, don't ya think?"

Hubert started moving away. He couldn't get out of there fast enough.

"Okay, okay, bad idea," Jane said as if to stop him. "But just imagine the benefits of not always having it covered up."

He bolted but noticed Leigh jump up after him.

CHAPTER 20

She stopped him at the cleaning station. Leigh pulled on Hubert's arm. He turned but didn't look at her. He couldn't. Every time something obscure happened, his only response was to get as far away as he could. The guy she was trying to create wouldn't do that. Hubert simply was not who she was looking for. How could she possibly be interested in taking this any further?

But she had chased after him which meant she wasn't giving up. She seemed willing to see this through, but after what had just happened, he wasn't sure he could trust her. Undoubtedly, this wouldn't be the last encounter for Hubert to face. He needed to be able to rely on someone: anyone. He'd thought that person would be Leigh. His confidence had just swelled because he knew she would be there for him. Now he wasn't so sure. Just as he wasn't the guy for her, she didn't seem right for him either.

"She's just nervous and a little OCD." Leigh forced him to look up. "Hey, you're rockin' this place."

Yeah, I was doing really well. Then I caved, right on queue. Just like all the other times.

"And, she's kinda right. I mean, everyone's seen it and talkin' about it." She touched his hand. "It's what sets you apart."

He bit his lip, careful with what he might say in the heat of the moment. He felt like coming out with it right then and there, just in line with the other bizarre conversation. But if anyone could make obscure comments seem right, it was Leigh. That may have given him some faith back, but he still didn't know if he could trust her. Could he trust her friends? That was a no-brainer.

"Perfect, my claim to fame is an uncut penis." He pulled away. *And for everyone involved, the penis will stay that way.*

That was the right decision, he thought, when it could have easily gone the other way. If he wanted everything to end right now, all he needed to do was start screaming about being circumcised. But she was here; she cared, and she seemed to want him as much as he wanted her. He probably could trust her, but the operation would stay with him. He wasn't in any position to trust anyone with that. Damn, he could barely trust himself.

"No, your claim to fame is a guy I met named Hubert

Rawlings. I want everyone to meet him."

"What if he's not who you think he is?"

"Then I'll become a *Bitch*." She got closer. "And from what I can see, you don't want that."

She couldn't have been more right. The last thing he wanted was to have to hook up with one of the *Bitches*, especially Virginia. And he definitely didn't want Leigh to fall into that group. He knew she didn't want that either. That's why she hung out with the obnoxious ones. She actually made excuses for their behavior just to keep from becoming a *Bitch*. Hubert started to understand that he'd been wrong. He might be the guy she was looking for, and she was just the type of girl he needed.

She took another step toward him, then closer. They were inches apart. This was another moment for him to escape, but he didn't this time. The urge was there: it was almost instinctive, but it was different this time. During all the other situations, it had been like he had no choice, but he didn't feel that way with Leigh. Not here, or in his bedroom really, or when he'd first met her in the storage room. Something about her calmed that anxiety.

"What is it you want, Hubert?"

He said nothing, but his eyes answered clearly: *you*.

She held his hands. "Who wouldn't want to be with the guy you're becoming? You're about to shatter my image of you."

He laughed slightly, knowing that image desperately

needed breaking. She smiled back with the confidence required to do just that.

"Go ahead. Show 'em the monster I've created. Show 'em the *Pubes Machine*."

CHAPTER 21

Will wasn't getting anywhere with his come-ons to the girl standing idly at Mark's cash register, or with his burger order from the guys working the grill. He turned back to the sitting area, frustrated.

At least before, he was never alone, and he could deflect all the rejection on someone else. Now he was beginning to think there was no point in him coming here at all. He had no purpose here: nothing to do and no friends. He saw Pubes cruising toward him.

He was relieved to see him, but really Pubes was just another source of disappointment. He knew Pubes was working and all that, but things seemed different today. For the first time, as far as Will knew, Pubes was actually part of the maintenance crew. They all seemed to be working together. Actually, they all seemed to be working for Pubes.

Something must have happened, which should be a good thing, but Will had a sneaking suspicion this wasn't going to work out in his favor. He had been watching Pubes, and the way he'd been moving out there just didn't seem right. Maybe it was just because Will wasn't with him. Possibly, Will was just being paranoid. It looked like Pubes had seen him, however, and he was making his way over to the counter Will stood at. He spruced up thinking Pubes actually did need the guaranteed, sidekick reassurance Will offered.

He watched Pubes make it to Chicken Fried Right's counter. Tyrell stopped him. Will saw Tyrell smile, huge.

"Hey, my man. Help a brother out," Tyrell said loud enough for Will to hear.

Tyrell forced a tray of fried chicken dishes into Pubes's hands. "It goes both ways, brother," Tyrell said.

Pubes appeared shocked and didn't know what to do with the tray. Will was much more resourceful. He started to move that way, but he was torn between helping Pubes and missing out on the order he'd been waiting so long for.

Tyrell turned Pubes around and suddenly became a midway carny. "Enjoy a fine selection of lunch offerings from Chicken Fried Right," Tyrell shouted.

Will watched Pubes stand there flustered. This was something Will could work with. He abandoned his order. He could come back in an hour, and it still wouldn't be ready, he thought. He slipped through the crowd and stood straight up, beside Pubes.

Will took a chicken nugget. He joined in on the sales pitch. "Looks right." He took a bite. "Tastes right." He pointed to the menu. "Priced right." He made an elaborate gesture to the store sign above.

Beside Pubes, Will's charm was back. He wasn't having any luck at Mark's counter, but here with Pubes, it was a different story. He quickly gained an audience. His voice was stronger; his movements were smoother. He winked at Tyrell and finished off the nugget.

Others around took interest in Chicken Fried Right. Tyrell postured up for orders.

Will asked Pubes, "You gonna eat this?" He would deal with Mark's burger later. This plate was solid and ready for eatin'. As soon as Pubes came along, man, things were looking up all ready, Will thought.

Will grabbed another nugget. "Let's sell this shit, baby." He moved away from the counter expecting Pubes to follow. In Will's mind, this show that Pubes starred in was about to elevate now that he was involved.

Unfortunately for Will, only he seemed to feel that way. Suddenly, Chester was with them. He didn't acknowledge Will at all. Will gulped his bite down not sure what to expect. Chester nudged Pubes.

"Drink down at Only Donut Holes," Chester said.

He gave Will a suspicious look which startled Will. It

wasn't a red carpet welcoming, but at least Will's existence was acknowledged.

Chester hurried away.

Will could see that Pubes was confused. Will knew he was considering staying right here. Even though Pubes was working, he would normally stay close to Will. At least Will expected that from Pubes, especially with Chester calling him on. But this time something was off.

Chester stopped before entering the sitting area with an impatient turn back.

Pubes pushed the tray to Will. "Maybe later."

Will was shocked. "Seriously?" He was being turned down for Chester? Will shook his head: confused. Pubes wouldn't abandon him just when he was about to get things rolling, would he? He watched Pubes reluctantly move away.

"I'm workin' here, Will."

Pubes joined up with Chester.

Will stood in the middle of a crowd that had formed at Chicken Fried Right. They had all come here in a matter of seconds, but no one was interested anymore. As quickly as the crowd appeared, they vanished. Will's flame had just started to burn but was suddenly snuffed out: just like the chicken snatched from Will's hands by Tyrell.

CHAPTER 22

Rand stood behind his counter while Drew flipped open two yellow *Wet Floor* signs. Tony started with the mop. If it was going to be a slow day selling donut holes, the entertainment these guys provided sure helped pass the time.

Shirley watched from behind her counter too. He asked her, "Shirley, you seen Danny?" He chomped down on a mouthful of salad and continued watching the clean-up action.

He wondered where these two got all their energy from. It was like Rod lined them all up downstairs and let them go like wind-up toys. It didn't matter what this crew had to do next, they always made a show of it and never disappointed. Rand looked at Shirley while she nursed a box of donut holes.

"You mean you haven't?" She didn't look back. The

Tony and Drew show was too much for her to turn away from.

He watched her pop a donut hole in her mouth. He considered how many donut holes Shirley had already consumed today. Even on a slow day, the ladies next door always kept the donut grease hot. Rand took another mouthful of salad. Suddenly, Hubert appeared on the scene with Chester which put Rand's attention back on the maintenance crew.

Magically, the area filled with fresh, young, potential customers. That was the beauty of this maintenance crew: they made everyone *cuckoo for donut holes*. Rand prepped up for business. "Great, just when I need him, he's nowhere."

"Here, Rand. You need to see this." Shirley slid him her cell phone.

A dude stepped up to Rand's counter. "Assorted box of holes please," he said, drawing on every word as though he'd forgotten what the next one should be.

Rand ignored the request. He was fixated on Shirley's cell phone. After looking at the first picture, he wrinkled his eyebrows. He hesitated before swiping the screen. His face stiffened; he swiped. He looked closer then swiped, and swiped, and swiped. Slowly, tentatively, he swiped another time. He kept staring at the phone. His eyeballs nearly touched the screen.

Danny suddenly appeared from the kitchen. Rand looked away from the phone to see him with his own flat-brimmed hat and shades. He looked ready to play the *Pubes* part, but his style was dated—extremely dated. He couldn't possibly be doing this, Rand thought. These kids were half his age, and none of them were... well, gay, at least as far as he knew.

Danny ignored Rand and directly went to serve the dude still standing at the other side of the counter. "A box full is asking a lot when one is usually enough." He sent the dude a sensual look. "Don't ya think?"

Rand watched Danny start to construct a box. Danny's eyes seemed anxious for the dude's response. He noticed the dude's phone lying face down on the counter.

"If you flip it over, I come wrapped too."

Rand was shocked by what Danny had just said—his Danny—and to a complete stranger no less. He scanned Shirley's phone again. He looked up to see the dude's head spinning side to side. Rand was totally embarrassed. He thought about pushing Danny out of the way and taking over, but it was probably too late for that. He saw the dude looking at Hubert, and slowly, the dude slipped into the crowd.

Danny glanced at Rand, but he turned away to serve the next customer.

***

Hubert stood dumbfounded among a growing swell of

admirers. Tony and Drew had the mess cleaned up, so he wasn't really needed there with Chester. He felt like the last cop arriving at an accident scene after the tow trucks had already arrived. Chester seemed fine with being a last responder, though. He did his best work with crowd control, and this *Pubes frenzy* was definitely going to need his expertise. Tony and Drew seemed eager to assist too. It was just Hubert who was having trouble with the swarm.

Hubert started to feel his reliable urge to get out quick. It was somehow different this time, though. It was nothing like when he only had Will to rely on. With Chester and the other two covering him, his anxiety settled quickly. Having these guys around insured Hubert that nothing was going to happen. They were taking all the attention, and Virginia was nowhere to be seen.

"Lunchtime, boys. Grab your weapon." Chester turned to Hubert. "Not literally, at least in public. Course, you don't have to worry about that." Chester put on his testosterone face.

Hubert wasn't catching on to Chester's comment other than it was lunchtime, and that was a good thing. The urge to flee wasn't as strong as before, but he was still uncomfortable. This would get him out of here unharmed: untouched.

Chester shrugged as though he needed a response. "Weapon… Lunch…"

Hubert smiled, slightly. If it wasn't frustrating enough having all these people around, trying to figure Chester out always had Hubert on edge. Chester could be dead serious or trying to be funny. Hubert never really knew for sure.

"I know, bad joke," Chester said.

"Actually, it's not even a joke," Drew said. "What would you call it, Tony?"

"Um, the word *weapon* used in place of *lunch*."

Chester shook his head. It seemed to Hubert that Chester felt the same way about these two.

"We eat over there, Pubes," Chester said a little deflated from trying to be the comedian.

"Sounds like an intentional reference to our new friend's source of popularity," Tony concluded.

"But it's not funny. Kinda threatening actually," Drew replied.

"You're right." Tony turned to Chester. "You're not funny, Chester.

Chester nodded with a disgusted look. "Right. Grab your, *lunch*." He pointed to an unoccupied table.

That instruction was again directed at Hubert, but Hubert was confused about how to respond, or if he should react at all. A smartass comment, like what Tony and Drew could get away with, would likely backfire big time. Just smiling and nodding was probably best at this point.

He looked to where Chester was pointing. The table

was empty and obviously staying that way, at least until these guys got there. All the tables around it were full, though. If they were selling tickets, even standing room only would be sold out. Not far away, Will sat alone with his burger.

***

Hubert stepped up to the crew's table, holding his faithful garden salad. At first he thought all the spots were taken. That was relieving because Will was still eating. There would be a place at his table, no doubt about that. He started to go there but saw one empty place, right in front of Chester. With his mouth full, Chester motioned for Hubert to take a seat.

Hubert hesitated. He looked over at Will. "Ahhh, I was going to—"

Chester coughed his food down. "Sit down. We…" He included everyone. "Need to talk." Chester licked his food away and took a drink. He wiped his mouth with his hand.

Hubert sat. He didn't have a choice. Will had seen him and was clearing the table to make room, but Chester's overbearing gaze made the decision clear. Hubert should have looked back, giving Will some type of indication that he was stuck, but he didn't. He couldn't bear to see Will's puppy dog sadness.

Chester didn't waste any time with his problem. In fact,

everyone sitting here seemed eager for Chester to continue.

"Okay, straight up. The hats are one thing, but I— we've got a problem."

Hubert shuffled nervously. He looked back to be sure he wasn't being surrounded. The last time, in the locker room, was bad enough. He could only imagine what these guys would do to him out here.

Even though no one was there, he wasn't going anywhere. The table alone had him trapped, and all the eyes around it pinned him down with no chance for escape.

"Oh, don't worry. It's not with you." Chester looked to the others. "Well, kinda. It's Virginia Almond actually." He turned sharply back to Hubert. "You know Virginia right?"

Hubert slowly nodded.

"It seems, Pubes, she wants your..." He smiled, provocatively. "I was gonna say ass, but that's not entirely accurate." He included everyone around with a wide arm sweep and turned up palms. "And we're good with that. It's not best case, but hey..."

Hubert took in another alluring smile. He snuck a peek at Will who was looking back, but clearly unaware of what Chester was talking about. Actually, Hubert wasn't exactly clear about where Chester was going with this either.

"Problem is, Pubes, you're taking all the others with her. We got nothin' left. That's not fair, right?"

Hubert shook his head.

"You're making it so damned hard, and really, Pubes, man, it's not necessary."

No, Chester, it's not. They're all yours; they always have been. Who am I to stand in your way? Hubert really wanted to say that, but for some reason the words wouldn't come out.

"But it's no problem. I got it fixed." Chester started to eat again. "We're gonna hook you up."

Great. Finally, I'll be free from this. The relief was amazing. Maybe he could convince Chester to include Will in his plan. He turned back to see what Will was doing. He was gone.

Wait—What? You're gonna do what?

"With Virginia."

Hubert's eyes popped. *With who?* His stare back at Chester should have cut right through him, but Chester didn't flinch.

Hubert looked to T-Woks. Leigh was not there either. The chair was still empty where Will had been. He searched frantically for one of them—anyone who could help him get away from here.

Chester picked something from a front tooth. "Tonight." Chester stopped with a forkful of food right in front of his mouth. He waited for a reaction.

Hubert's expression froze, like the temperature just dropped fifty degrees. He could feel himself starting to shake. His face must have lost all its color since Hubert felt like his blood had stopped circulating.

Every other time the *Pubes* act had taken him to a point like this, he was able to shake everyone off and get away. This time was different, though—extremely different. This time he was in with the maintenance crew. They all thought they were helping Hubert, but indirectly, they were working for themselves. There was no way Hubert would be able to slip out of this. He was in it for the long haul with a sexually motivated crew, and the hungry man train rolled *tonight*.

Hubert looked away from Chester. He saw his own hands trembling. He needed to say something to defend himself, but he couldn't talk before and definitely not now. He didn't know what to say anyway. The only thing he could do is try to act cool and make it look like nothing fazed him. But it was Hubert Rawlings who needed to do this, and everything bothered him. He may have fooled these guys so far, but what they wanted from him now was far beyond his capabilities.

He took a deep breath and looked back at Chester. He tried for words, but nothing came out. He needed to calm down first. He looked at his hands again. They were visibly shaking.

Chester chomped down on his fork. "Eat up. Your salad's gettin' cold."

CHAPTER 23

Will thumbed through samples while he stood alone at the Beautiful Brilliance Kiosk. Behind him, the food court was nearly empty. That wasn't because anything had drastically changed here. It was just late, and the mall was about to close. On any other day, Will would be gone by now too, but today he felt lost in abandonment. Only the kiosk offered him any kind of comfort.

Will hadn't left since he was basically dumped by Pubes in favor of greener pastures. He didn't blame Pubes. The whole goal was to get in deep with the maintenance crew, and Pubes had done that. The only problem was that Will should have been included. Either Pubes had ignored that small detail, or Will himself had failed to pull that part off.

With everything happening so fast, Will couldn't put his finger on who was at fault. Probably, blame wasn't the issue, though. He remembered the look on Pubes's face the last time he'd seen him. Pubes definitely intended to eat lunch with him. Will had thought that Pubes was simply stuck with those guys, but maybe that look was something else. Maybe, Pubes's confusion had been over the popularity Chester and the boys offered versus the obscurity Will had always given him.

Having spent the rest of the afternoon, and the whole evening here, Will concluded that Pubes had chosen fame over fear. Why wouldn't he? Those guys had so much to offer that Will couldn't. The fright that always guided Pubes to Will's side was obviously not an issue now. It looked like Pubes had found a new source of protection, and from the rumors swirling around the food court, Will thought Pubes may have finally confronted his demons.

This made Will think about where it left him. If he didn't do something about it, he would have no one. That was something Will had never considered until now. Pubes had been loyal to him since they first met in grade school. It had always been Pubes who was dependent on Will. He had never thought of Pubes as the type who would leave him like this, but it looked like Pubes was abandoning him. Soon, Will would be on his own, just like he was now.

He looked back into the food court. It was empty. Will felt vacant too. This feeling was new to him, but he quickly shook that thought away. None of this would get Will back on track with his plan. Pubes knew this was all

Will's dream. If anything, Pubes should simply pass the torch. How could Pubes possibly continue on and not bring Will along for the ride?

Somehow, none of it made sense. At least Will refused to let it make sense. That seemed to be the only way to get himself back into this game. He needed to keep thinking. He needed to get close to Pubes again. That shouldn't be too hard. Finding a way to make a difference would be the challenge. That exact situation had always tested Will, which mostly ended up in failure; but he was not the type who would give up trying.

The kiosk owner started to close his shutters. Will grabbed a couple of samples and turned away: face-to-face with Leigh.

"Beware, for the junk food of skin care," Leigh said with her Chinese drawl.

Will chuckled, but he wasn't into it. "You're not as scary as you used to be." He continued on, past her and away from the food court.

Leigh stayed with him. "Neither are you." She touched his hair and smelled her fingers. "I make you delish," she said.

"And alone." Will kept walking. He really didn't mean to make it sound like any of this was Leigh's fault, but he didn't feel like backtracking on that statement either.

Leigh stopped, abruptly. She pulled him back by the arm. Oh shit, Will thought. Just after he'd spent most of the day beating himself up, now he was going to have to sugarcoat his harsh choice of words. He was too tired for that. All he wanted to do was leave, but Leigh seemed to be up for a fight. When he looked at her, however, she didn't appear fazed by the comment at all.

"I doubt it, Will. He's not the type to go solo."

Will turned away from her. "Well, I guess you've wrapped him up to complete the package."

Damn, another shot right in the gut. Will was fully aware that he couldn't keep doing this. Two times he might get away with, but a third... Knowing Leigh the way he did, three times would likely make him part of the product display they were standing in front of.

Leigh hesitated, obviously aware of Will's bitterness. He figured she was biting inside her mouth to hold back from blasting him. Her mind seemed to be on Pubes, though.

Will noticed her hesitation, so he continued before she had a chance to blast him. "Our boy Pubes is about to break new ground."

Leigh tilted her head a little. "What's that supposed to mean, Will?"

He couldn't believe she didn't know what he was talking about. The rumors had been spreading through the food court all afternoon. The possibility of Leigh not knowing seemed so remote. She had eyes all over this place. Between her and her friends... Maybe she knew more than everyone else, which actually made more sense than the rumor itself.

"Well, Chester's set it up. If anyone could, it would be him."

She obviously still didn't get it. Will stepped back, shocked.

"Chester's set up what?"

"Really? You don't know about this?" Will paused expecting Leigh to cave into her own naivety. She would no doubt come clean on her knowledge of Pubes's big, upcoming moment, putting Will straight into the hole he'd already dug for himself.

Oh, what the hell, he thought. Humor her. "The hookup." He might as well play along. What difference would it make?

"A hookup. With who?"

He shook his head. She really didn't know what this was all about. That meant Will was not the last person to find out. It didn't mean much, but it did a whole lot to lift Will's spirit.

"Virginia," Will said almost as though it was his victory.

"Says who?"

"Chester. I told you. Chester's set it up."

Will could see Leigh didn't believe it, or she didn't want to believe it. She was processing the whole idea right in front of him. He could tell she was accusing herself. She'd created the guy Pubes was now, and she should have known Chester would do something like this.

"Where?"

She asked that while she was still thinking: no doubt trying to come up with a solution. But even though she blamed herself for what Pubes couldn't handle; and Will was stuck trying to figure out how he could get involved, they were both standing here. They were possibly the only ones left out. So what went down tonight wouldn't involve them: something neither of them were comfortable with.

Will moved away. "I wasn't invited."

Leigh pulled him back. He could see the determination in her eyes. She started all of this, and there was no way she wasn't going to get a say in what was coming next.

"Neither was I," she said.

CHAPTER 24

Hubert staggered a little then fell back, stopped only by his locker. In front of him, the room was alive like everyone there had just won a championship.

From lunch, with Chester and the rest of the crew, until now was a complete blur to Hubert. What happened after lunch; where he went after his shift; how he got into this shape... He couldn't remember any of it. At this point, none of that mattered anyway. Just trying to stand straight and see clearly was all he could concentrate on.

He watched booze flow freely from cup to cup. He tried to focus on everything, but it was much easier to watch the cups. They were red and active, like little red dots decorating the room.

The more he concentrated on them, the more it seemed like they were floating. They moved up and down. They came together then dashed apart. They rose high and tilted; they turned upside down and smashed to the ground.

Suddenly, Hubert realized he held one too. He looked at it. He tilted his head slightly, realizing this thing was responsible for how he felt. Understanding that was a lot to ask considering he was new to all of this, but the rules seemed simple enough. All he had to do was drink from it, and everything was fine.

Everyone responsible for his sudden grief was here with him, but they weren't any problem now. *Amazing.* He continued to stare at the cup he held. He wavered from the locker and lifted the empty cup high in the air.

He cleared his throat. He opened his eyes wide. "Here's to Chester," Hubert said, barley able to get the words out.

He was shocked that the room quieted as soon as he spoke. Everyone turned to him. Just with the words *here's to Chester.* He looked at the red cup he held high above him. *Umm, magic in a little red cup.*

"Now there's a guy who's—" Hubert struggled to find his words. "One big dick."

Everyone chuckled, but Hubert didn't see any of them. He only saw Chester spin around quickly, spilling half his drink.

"Ummm. Try again." He blinked, trying to get Chester's face in focus. "Chester's—" He paused again for clarity. "The biggest dick I've ever seen."

Chester stepped up.

"Oh wow." Hubert gave Chester a cockeyed smile even though Chester was close enough to pop him. "Can't forget the *got*." Hubert reached for him with his cup. "Chester, my man, of all the dicks, you've—" Hubert staggered back. He closed his eyes then popped them open, wide. "The biggest."

Chester's drink dropped. He primed himself for a pounding.

Hubert saw that Chester was steaming. He knew what his cocked arm could do, but he did nothing to get away. In super slow motion, Chester's fist approached. It went from blurry, to crystal clear, to a memory as it whizzed by his head. The crashing sound of fist on metal was deafening, inches from Hubert's ear.

Hubert vaguely noticed a fight circle forming. "What? You've all seen the picture. Buddy's hung huge," Hubert said.

Chester backed off.

"What can I say?" Hubert took a big, empty drink.

Drew cruised by, and Hubert's drink was full again. Hubert motioned to thank him, but Drew was gone before any words came out.

Just then, Virginia appeared with the Bitches in tow. Up until now, Hubert was fine with everyone around him. But Virginia presented an extremely different situation. If he remembered correctly—which he was having trouble doing—this whole event, down here in the locker room,

173

was set up by Chester. All of it done for Hubert to hook up with Virginia…

"Yeah, Yeah. We all know where to go if it's size you're lookin' for," Virginia said.

She zeroed in on Hubert, and he knew it. He looked for a way out, but that didn't seem likely.

"Me, I prefer originality."

Hubert may have been drunk, but he wasn't incoherent, yet. He looked at everyone looking at him, then at his drink. He downed it.

"You *bitches* pick your candy. This lollypop is mine."

Virginia closed in. "The thousand words I got from that picture ain't tellin' me the whole story."

That message was presented directly at Hubert. He moved away from the locker. He took a few steps without taking his eyes off Virginia. She followed him cunningly. He stopped suddenly. Something blocked him from going further. Nothing, or no one, was stopping Virginia, though. At this point, it was just him and her.

He gulped as she approached. Hubert fell back on a bench.

***

Apprehensively, Leigh pushed on the locker room door from the hallway. She had expected the door to be locked, or at least shut to keep in the noise, but neither was the case. It was open a crack allowing her and Will to enter without a problem.

Immediately, she saw Elle and Jane there, each wrapped under the arm of their favorite jaw breaker. *They knew about this and didn't say anything...* Leigh caught their eyes: busted.

She looked around, shocked about how this could be going on without her knowing. She saw Will looking too. He was obviously unconcerned about not being invited. His face glowed with satisfaction. The fact that he was here was certainly good enough for him.

"How about some live action, Pubey baby," Leigh heard someone say.

There were too many people in front of her to see what was going on, but she knew where the voice came from. She was also quite sure who said it.

Leigh hesitated to go any further.

***

Will wasn't as timid. The door he had just come through was simply too close to him. He could easily be pushed back into the hallway, so he went for a front row seat.

He'd heard the comment, just like Leigh had, but Will was shocked to see Virginia making sensual contact then straddle Pubes, lap dance style. Will had only seen this type of stuff in select movies he watched by himself. This time, however, he had a live act in front of him with Pubes as the leading man.

Pubes's head snapped back. Will could see his eyes starting to swim. Pubes looked away from Virginia shaking his head, as if he was trying to say no, or... It actually looked like Pubes was trying to stay awake.

Will couldn't believe what he was seeing. He knew Pubes better than anyone here, and Will could definitely tell Pubes was about to pass out. He shook his head, totally shocked. How could Pubes possibly be thinking of sleep at a time like this? Then he noticed all the red cups. Everyone there had one except him and Leigh. Actually, Virginia didn't either, but Pubes still held on to one tightly. He had a death grip on it.

Will watched Virginia gently guide Pubes's head back for eye contact. She grabbed his crotch.

His eyes popped like popcorn. Will's eyes popped more. Will turned to Leigh who was standing beside him. This was true entertainment for Will but not for Leigh.

She looked at Will. He could tell she'd had enough. She turned away shaking her head and headed for the door. Will watched her go, but he stayed put.

Sure, feel free to abandon our friend when he needs us the most. Leigh had only known Pubes for a few weeks, so it made sense for her to bolt. He, on the other hand, had been Pubes's best friend forever. *There's no way I'm going to miss*

176

any of this—I mean, going to leave him in this mess.

Will stepped in for a closer look. Pubes's head swirled in a sea of confusion. He blinked rapidly, desperate for a solution. He looked right at Will, but Will could tell nothing was registering.

Then he was out, cold: down for a double eight count.

Will's head snapped back. *He was falling asleep. Talk about wrong man for the job.* But all Will could do at this point was get his fighter back in the ring.

He noticed Virginia was shocked, but she didn't dismount.

"Chester, quick! I need a lesson in coma sex," Virginia shouted.

Will looked around while he moved toward them. Everyone watching was close to the action. Will saw Chester take the shot with pride.

"Just let the poor boy sleep, Virg. With you on top, I know how he feels," Chester said.

Touché, Will thought. He chuckled along with everyone else.

"I'm kinda wondering how he feels myself," Virginia said.

Will watched her squeeze his crotch. She started to unzip his zipper. Will cringed at the thought of it all.

The crowd ramped up for action.

She pulled open his pants. Both her hands were ready to yank on the waist.

Everyone went nuts.

Will stepped back. There was nothing he could do for Pubes now. He would literally get trampled from the frenzy if he tried to intervene. Why would he want to anyway? Magic was about to happen for Pubes even if he wasn't awake for it. He would be a legend after this.

Will watched her pull but not hard enough. Pubes didn't move. She dismounted for more leverage. She pulled again, and the pants were off.

Silence. There was nothing but shocked faces all around. At first Will had no idea why. He saw Virginia go in for a closer look.

"A fuckin' scam!" She looked up to find Chester. "Bastard! Where's the jacket, Chester? I shoulda guessed."

Chester was shocked too. Now, Will caught on. There was no jacket; no sleeve; no cover for the power driver that teed this whole situation up.

Pubes moved. His eyes were rolling behind closed lids. He moved with soft groans. What the fuck, Will thought. Is he going to wake up or what?

The crowd ignited again. A chant started. "Up, up, up…"

No, it couldn't be… Will suddenly realized he really needed to wake Pubes up. He reached out, but Virginia started playing an invisible flute, like a snake charmer. She got closer, too close.

Pubes moved. He groaned again.

The chant…

Virginia…

Suddenly silence, again, followed by groans and muffled laughter.

Everyone went hysterical.

Will snapped back at the same time Virginia did. She held out her dripping hands.

Will heard Girls shriek with disgust.

***

Hubert sprung to life. His eyes were alive at the sight of being surrounded. Virginia's shocked eyes stared straight at his. Her arms were up, like she was being busted.

She screamed!

CHAPTER 25

Will's face was the first thing Hubert was able to focus on. He was having trouble figuring out exactly what had just happened. Will's expression told him it wasn't good, and Will's determination to get him moving said there wouldn't be any time to dwell on it.

"Pubes, get up! We gotta roll," Will said.

Hubert tried to follow Will's rapid head movements, but he settled on Chester busting a gut with the rest of the crew. They were all staring, and pointing below Hubert's waist. He looked down...

He'd been in this exact room with his pants around his ankles before, but something about this was definitely not right. The shock of it all didn't allow him to process everything fast enough before Will had him sitting up.

"Fuck, man, if you don't move now you'll be headline news," Will said.

Will pulled up Hubert's pants and had him starting for the door. Hubert's first steps were influenced by the lingering effects of alcohol and his undone pants. He had seen the urgency in Will's face, though, so there was no use second guessing what they were fleeing from.

Virginia screamed, "What the fuck!?"

Hubert saw Will cringe in front of him. The scream almost stopped him dead in his tracks. Fleeting thoughts about what had happened rushed through Hubert's head, but he couldn't possibly put it all together. The door was their destination, but it was still too far away. Will surged for it.

"Chester!"

Will turned back to Hubert; Hubert turned back to Virginia. He watched her practically fly across the room at Chester.

"Do something!" she screamed at him. Her fists pounded Chester's chest.

Just then Hubert locked eyes with Chester. Despite not being able to comprehend what went on in here, he knew Chester and Virginia were involved. At this point, neither of them seemed pleased with the results. If the room wasn't already spinning enough, Chester's surge toward him put it into a full scale T5 Tornado.

He turned back to Will. Will had the door open and lunged to grab Hubert's arm. Will pulled him through as Hubert took one last look back. The room had gone insane.

Hubert staggered in the hallway and fell back against the wall. "Will." He was relieved that only Will was with him. He grabbed for him. "What happ—"

"Forget the past, pal," Will said.

Hubert heard a stampede approaching the door. Will pulled it shut.

"We need to work on a short-term plan," Will said.

He pulled on Hubert to get him moving. Will's urgency couldn't have been stronger, but Hubert refused to budge. He had to get his head straight before moving any further.

"What happened, Will?"

He remembered Virginia straddling him; the chaos, and his confusion. At first it was all too much for him to handle, but all of the sudden everything else had been blocked out. It was just him and Virginia, like the dreams he had about her in the storage room. This time, however, she wasn't too far away. She was all over him. All he could do was enjoy the moment.

"The moist spot in your boxers should refresh your memory," Will said.

That realization broke him from the fantasy, just like his sudden wake up had. He realized what all the commotion was about, and embarrassment quickly set in.

The door burst open.

"But now's not the time for memories," Will said with his sense of urgency back, full throttle.

This time Hubert had no choice. Will moved him along faster than his feet could keep up.

"It didn't work. I told her it wouldn't work." Hubert shook his head slowly.

He tried to stop running; he tried to get his balance. He struggled to get his pants done up.

"Keep movin', Pubes."

He rounded a corner with Will behind him making sure he kept on track. Hubert saw the Only Donut Holes door opened into the hallway. He swung past it. Rand and Danny were arguing in the doorway.

"What the fuck does she know about these things anyway?" Hubert picked up the pace.

His legs pounded the concrete, but his mind couldn't have been further from what motivated that. If anything, he was running from his mother.

The thought of his mother caused him to burn even faster through the narrow hallway. A vision of Tung stacking boxes of T-Woks hats blurred by.

"But no, no. She wouldn't listen."

He saw Will keeping up and looking at him as though he was nuts. Will's mouth moved; his arms pumped, and he looked back down the hallway they'd fled through. Hubert didn't care about any of that, though.

"She's crazy, Will. I tell ya..." Hubert's eyes bulged with insanity. "My mother's crazier than..." He suddenly saw the chaotic trail they had left behind. "Steaming bulls in a narrow hallway."

He finally realized the sense of urgency Will had been trying to enforce. Will had moved ahead, so Hubert quickly picked up his pace.

Javier crossed the hallway right in front of them. He carried stacks of taco shells. He stopped like he was stuck in oncoming traffic.

Hubert tried to pull Will back, but it was too late. Three guys and tacos flew.

Struggling to get his feet back under him, Hubert saw the gang of linebackers racing to the accident scene.

Will yanked on Hubert's arm, and suddenly, a door opened beside him. Will lunged for it, and pulled Hubert through.

CHAPTER 26

The door shut on its own with a mechanical click. Hubert was still messed up with all the urgency, but the sequence of events were slowly piecing themselves together. He saw Will looking around, gathering his thoughts. It was quiet: peacefully quiet, and apparently safe. Judging by the looks of Will, though, Hubert doubted things would stay this way.

Hubert knew what happened with Virginia in the locker room. He shook his head after realizing how humiliating this would be for him. He'd protected himself for so long from anyone finding out about those dreams. He figured nobody knew. Not Will; not his mother... He had been shocked when his mother hit him with the news about the circumcision. Not only because of the drastic operation, but also because she was so open about it all.

Her little talks after the announcement were intended

to relieve the stress, but she was so aware of his wet dreams. She'd even convinced him, a little, that these fantasies would go away after the operation. It would leave him with dreams like everyone else had, not tangled up in sexual adventures that always ended abruptly with sticky boxers. Secretly, he looked forward to that.

"And I thought she was a saint," Hubert said.

Hubert hung his head realizing she was just his crazy mother, obsessed with a crazy idea to solve her son's crazy imagination. Now a video would no doubt emerge. A picture got him into this mess; a video would finish him off for good. He wondered if Will had a plan for that. He looked up. Instead of seeing Will as he expected, Leigh was there.

But why? She wasn't in the locker room as far as Hubert knew. Neither was Will for that matter. He kind of remembered seeing her friends, though. Will was definitely there when he woke up, so she must have been with him.

Had she opened the door? If that was the case, she would have known he was running from something in the hallway. If she knew he was running, she probably knew why. He closed his eyes and gulped. And if she knew why, she must have seen everything.

When he opened his eyes, she was still there. He could see the disappointment in her face. In fact, it looked like she'd been crying. She was too far away, but he was pretty sure he had seen tears on her face. He stepped toward her.

She hesitated, then disappeared around the corner.

Suddenly, the dark quietness was replaced with pounding at the door. He wanted to chase after her, but he knew in seconds it would be him being chased, again. He looked at the door. It wasn't opening. The handle shook violently.

He saw Will desperately looking for an escape route. Will didn't have a plan for any of this. That was obvious. Hubert reached for him to get moving when he saw Mark leaning against a stack of bread trays, calmly smoking a joint.

He offered it to Hubert.

***

Chester and the rest of the crew raged an all-out assault on the door that was now shut tight. Chester stepped back, frustrated that he had to give up. He looked away and saw a touch pad on the wall.

Chester was first to burst through the door with the others almost plowing him over. He held them back.

"Got him!"

He saw that little bastard with his back turned, and it looked like he was desperately hiding something. Chester tilted his head and wrinkled his brow. Shouldn't he be running? Fuck it, Chester thought. He plowed forward for a grand body tackle.

Shocked, Mark turned. His reefer glowed with a huge header. Instinctively, he swallowed it whole.

Two inches from Mark's face, Chester realized his mistake. He twitched, but refrained from impact.

Mark gulped.

Chester backed off, frustrated. He looked around realizing Pubes was gone. He kicked some nearby boxes then went ballistic on them. The others stepped back and let him have it out with the cardboard.

Chester finished after realizing this was getting him nowhere. He still had Virginia to deal with, and Pubes wasn't under his arm to make that go easier. At this point he would have to try a different approach. Possibly, his charm like every other time. He blinked trying to erase the stress from his face.

He went back to the door. It was locked. He pounded it. "Fuck!" He turned back to see Mark holding a key card.

Mark smiled. He hiccupped a puff of smoke.

CHAPTER 27

Hubert walked slowly with Will in the night's silence. When he'd fled from the back of the mall, he hoped he would find Leigh. The prospect of Chester and the crew bursting through those doors sent him and Will, who knows where. He looked around to figure out where he was. She must have run off in a different direction because she was nowhere to be seen now.

Being here with Will was probably best anyway. If he did find Leigh, what would he say to her? He couldn't explain what happened in there; he didn't know how it happened himself. Actually, having Will beside him sucked too. What type of explanation will he be looking for? He really wished he was alone.

"Really, Pubes, it's not that bad."

Hubert kept moving with his head down. *It's not that bad because it didn't happen to you.*

191

"Personally, I'm impressed. Are you kiddin' me? Performance under pressure like that."

Hubert didn't react. A reaction of any type would only encourage Will to talk more. At this point Hubert didn't care for any of his comments. Nothing coming out of Will's mouth would solve any of this, so silence was what Hubert hoped for.

"A shocker in the locker room."

Hubert made like he didn't hear him.

"A blusher gusher."

Hubert shook his head realizing silence at a time like this, from a guy like Will, simply would not happen.

"A cream dream with Virginia the Food Court Queen."

Hubert kept walking. Will had to catch on eventually that the jokes weren't helping. But, actually, they were distracting Hubert from the reality of what just happened. This was the great thing about having Will for a friend. He never took things too seriously. Everything seemed to just roll off him, and Hubert could usually ride the same wave away from their problems. This time, Hubert wasn't so sure he could do that.

Will stopped him, briskly. "And what actually did happen to the famous cock cover?"

Hubert cringed. That was the other thing about Will. He had no filter. Subtlety was not in his DNA, but that was a question Hubert had asked himself over and over. Maybe not quite so directly, but how he ended up like this continued to baffle him. "She said, 'It's all about sensitivity, dear. I certainly don't want you to do like Daddy does.'" Hubert shook his head, disgusted that he'd let it happen. "I'm a kid who can't even have his own dreams."

Finally, Will stopped talking. Hubert could see he was taking a second to think this through. In the past, nothing seemed too bizarre for Will. He was the king of absurdity, but this was possibly too much for even him to process.

"Your mother, Norma? You mean she made you get cut because of your nightly adventures?" He wrinkled his face and cupped his head in his hands. "And Daddio just stood there letting the knives fly?"

Hubert turned away and walked. The realization of it all was simply too much. There was too much talking; too much thinking. This night had gotten to the point of no return, and Will was only making things worse. Hubert had to get away and deal with this on his own.

"It's fuckin' sick, man. No, not sick…"

Hubert could see Will prepping for the closer. He didn't get one. Will sighed. He stayed with Hubert, though. They walked in silence for a while. *At least he's getting the point.*

"I tell ya, she's crazy, man." Will shook his head.

Hubert sighed. *Well, maybe not.*

"A fuckin' Mad Momma. They're both nasty insane." Will thought about it for a second. "You're bloody lucky it

193

didn't work. Can't take the dreams away, it's the only thing we've got."

He might as well have been talking to himself. He was really, but Will didn't seem to care. It was obvious this was getting personal for Will. In his silence, he had probably put himself in Hubert's shoes.

"And no changes coming anytime soon by the looks of it." Will went back into silent mode. But that likely wouldn't be for long, like a wounded soldier refusing to die. "Damn, she cut away my only wish."

"I only wish she didn't walk away," Hubert said quietly.

Will snapped out of his rant. "Who walked away? Leigh?"

Damn, I shouldn't have said that. I should have let him go on about feeling sorry for himself. That way, I won't get involved in another crazy plan. Involving Leigh will only spin Will off in another direction that would no doubt involve me in the master plan. Damn! I should have kept my mouth shut. I should have walked away a long time ago. I should have never listened to Will, and his food court hiring plan, in the first place.

"You can't fault a girl who prefers some acting and a decent plot," Will said.

So she was there; she was with him. "What did she see?" *If he's not going to stop talking, I might as well find out what I'm up against.*

"Who cares? She saved our asses."

Hubert stopped as if he'd suddenly run out of

pavement. "Then she walked. She looked me straight in the eyes. She was disgusted with what she saw, so she walked."

"She helped us get what we want, so what's the problem?"

Hubert looked Will over with tight lips. For some reason he was holding back what he should have said a long time ago. He had always felt Will's way of thinking was right, though. They were young and stuff like this shouldn't mean so much, but Hubert always dwelled on the risk. Why couldn't he just appreciate what she had done for them? She helped them get in with the food court crew; she helped them escape from the same guys; what else could they expect from her?

From Will, nothing. But *she* expected more from Hubert. She helped him break out of his shell, and she wanted more. She didn't want more from Will, she wanted it from Hubert. So when Will said, *she helped us get what we want,* the word *we* didn't apply.

"Get what *you* want," Hubert said.

"And what's wrong with that?"

Hubert turned to confront Will. He could lay into him right here and now, but what good would it do. This was the way Will thought, and he was probably better off. At least he didn't worry about everything. At least he could move on without drowning in the past. Getting a life lesson from a seventeen-year-old wouldn't do anything to change him. Venting about Will being a better person wouldn't change this mess. Hubert backed off.

"For you, Will, I wouldn't expect anything else. For me..." He looked away, embarrassed. "I'm a fraud, so she walked."

"If she walked, it's not because of your penis or your T-Woks hat. It's because you changed. At least to her you did."

Hubert popped his head up. *Wow! Where did that come from? Maybe there was some depth in this shallow person I know as Will.*

"Into what, Will? I'll tell you what. Into someone I could never be. Someone I don't want to be."

"So you took it a bit too far. Just back off a little."

And use you as an example?

"I don't know what the big deal is," Will said.

Well, how about this. Like you said, I took it too far; and like always, you can't take it far enough. "But I don't want to change at all, Will. That's what I've been trying to tell you." Hubert yanked up his pants and pulled the belt tight. "It's what *you* want."

Will nodded. Hubert could tell he was actually getting this. He doubted Will was going to miraculously agree, but he was at least capable of understanding. Their problem still existed, though. Hubert just then realized how far apart he was from his best friend.

"But it's what we both need. We can't just sit around

pretending to enjoy being losers," Will said.

"I kinda liked the loser I was." Hubert took off his T-Woks hat and pushed it to Will. "Guess you didn't."

Hubert moved away. He figured Will would follow, but this time he didn't. He actually expected Will to stay with him, but this was better. He needed to be alone.

"What about Leigh? Does she like Hubert Rawlings?"

Hubert looked at him, but he didn't answer. He took off in another direction.

***

Instinctively, Will began to follow Pubes, but he stopped. There didn't seem to be any point. Will knew all of this was on Pubes. He made sure it went that way. It had always worked out, and look at both of them now. They had evolved, which never would have happened if it wasn't for Will.

He nodded while taking credit, even if it was only in his mind. He knew Pubes was smart enough to see the whole picture. It was just a matter of time before he realized it. In the end, if Pubes didn't see the light—shit, Will was a new man now. He could do it alone if it came down to that.

Will looked at the hat. "I don't need a hat," he said as though Pubes was still there with him.

He reshaped his hair knowing he had it all figured out.

He looked at his hand. He started to wipe it on his pants but licked it instead.

He watched Pubes rounding a corner in the distance.

CHAPTER 28

Will turned into the same thriving jungle of youth this food court had been before. All of the madness Pubes had created was gone, though. There were no more timid unknowns; no more chasing private parts; no more T-Woks hats. The food court had a social hierarchy, and everyone here had their old job back. It was only Will who seemed to have missed the memo.

Will cruised through the eating section, still trying to shop his image. Even though he was on his own, he wasn't about to give up just because Pubes had. Will could feel it. A breakthrough for him was coming, but once again, he was only able to impress himself. He stopped and raised his shades. He looked around for something, someone.

There wasn't a lot for Will to work with. Even as Pubes's sidekick, he'd always been transparent here. They had worked this floor together with Will leading the way most of the time. Eyes were never on him, though. But to Will, he was part of that show. Even if the main attraction was missing in action, Will wasn't going anywhere.

This may have turned into a one man gig, but Will was just the type to make it his. His focus had to be getting in with the maintenance crew. That's what Pubes had done. How could Will do the same? Pubes had the opportunity of a lifetime with them. Will would have given just about anything to be in Pubes's place in that locker room.

He placed his shades, determined to make this work. He continued to work his swagger, but his potential fans seemed too busy to notice him at all. *Surely, someone in here sees me.* He tried harder with food line interruptions and exaggerated hip swings around tables. After little success, he stopped short of total embarrassment. He sighed.

Will stepped up to a dejected Tyrell at Chicken Fried Right. He had seen Tyrell watching him: one of the few. Since no one was paying attention to either of them, Will figured misery attracts. Tyrell couldn't sell any chicken; Will couldn't sell himself. He doubted Tyrell would have any miracle cures, but a little wound licking probably wouldn't hurt.

Tyrell asked, "What the hell happened to my cover man? I thought we had a deal?"

Will looked down, defeated. "Trust me, I know."

Tyrell tapped the sale button on his cash register. An empty cash tray popped open. "This was overflowin' with—"

"Hey, man, I'm sinking here too. You're not the only one who needs bailing out."

Will didn't have any answers, but he could tell Tyrell's gears were turning. He looked Will up and down. *That's right. Put a tray in my hands and watch the chicken fry.* But there wasn't a sample tray in sight. Will looked beyond Tyrell for something he may have missed. *Damn, nothing. You should know I'm not too proud to come right out with it.* Will gave Tyrell a *here it comes* look.

"So you're tellin' me we're in this together?"

"Hell, yeah, like my gut needs your Drum Stick Platter," Will said. Sure, their motivation was set on completely different targets, but two working it was better than one. He may not be another Pubes, but there had to be some value in an inside man like Tyrell. If nothing else, he came with unlimited chicken combos…

Will scanned the overhead menu. *No harm in getting familiar with the menu options.* He made sure Tyrell didn't miss his intent.

"And you've got a direct line to this boy, Pubes?"

"Not if I have to work on an empty stomach."

Tyrell snapped his fingers for some action behind him. "Well, then, let's get this boy all fueled up."

Augh, finally some respect. It's not quite what I was lookin' for, but everyone's got to start somewhere. Will smiled knowing lunch was about to be served.

***

Will sat all alone, but he was content with his Chicken Fried Right fix. His drive to succeed on the popularity front would simply have to wait. Will had set his priorities to capitalize on his new image, but strength and energy would be required to sustain the effort. This new found source of fuel was quickly finding a way into the timeline.

With his mouth full, he saw Italy's Best doing some decent business. Not everyone was suffering in this place, but it seemed strange that pizza slices were outselling chicken wings ten to one.

Sub Attack moved through a line of hungry patrons by building assembly line sandwiches. Between those two stores, Mark Saint John's Fried Burgers had a long line, but Mark and his staff struggled to get their shit together.

Will figured surging demand and plummeting sales were just part of the competition here, but who was he to care about the economics of the food court. He had a piece of the action in front of him. For now, things were looking up for Will. At least he wasn't going to end up being hungry.

Will turned to see Salads Like Mom Makes serving female clientele while Rand struggled at Only Donut Holes to fill orders by himself.

Throughout all of this, Pubes was nowhere to be seen.

Just having him appear would solve all of Will's problems, but it looked like Pubes had gone back in hiding. Will knew where he was this time. All he had to do was knock on that dreaded door again. Maybe he would have to do that, but for now, Will was busy.

He gnawed on a drumstick and noticed Tyrell staring a hole into him. Tyrell seemed impatient to get results from his new found marketing strategy. Surely he didn't expect Pubes to instantly appear. Will wasn't sure if Pubes would ever come back, but he was already chewing on his payment for making that happen. Will looked at the drumstick then back to Tyrell.

Will looked to T-Woks. There was no business there either despite all the hats Tung had setup for sale. Also missing at T-Woks was Leigh. She might know what was up with Pubes, but Will seriously doubted it. If she'd had any contact with Pubes, he certainly would have. If anything, she was gone for good from here too.

Will took a second look. Leigh could definitely help him, though. She had before, so she probably would again. If it was for no other reason than to get Pubes back here, that would work for Will. He saw that as a double bonus, but finding her looked like it might be a problem. He started to scan the crowd again.

Virginia was with her Bitches. The maintenance crew performed. Will watched them for a while and noticed their act was without Chester. That was definitely strange.

Whenever the maintenance crew worked their magic, Chester was always there to work the crowd. Will had never seen it any other way except for now.

Will put down his chicken. He looked deeper. Finding Chester wouldn't help him, but both he and Leigh missing didn't make sense. That thought spiked Will's curiosity. He stood up a little after he thought he saw something. *Augh, just wishful thinking.* He turned back to the drumstick. *Could that have been Chester?* He looked again. Sure enough, it was him, at the door by the washrooms.

Chester opened the door and looked around secretively. Will could tell he was up to something. He'd never seen Chester peeping around corners at the food court. Chester was the life of this place. Now he seemed to be hiding from it. Suddenly, Leigh appeared and slipped through the door.

Wow, Will thought. He sunk down in his chair, trying to hide from nothing really. *That was weird.* She was always behind the counter at T-Woks, but she was just with Chester? Will remembered Leigh saying she knew Chester, but he never thought they were secretly hanging out. Will thought about what he'd just seen. Yeah, there was no mistake about it. They were definitely hanging out, and whatever they were doing, it was being done secretly.

Suddenly, Chester followed her, and the door shut tight.

Will jumped up not sure what to do. He looked back to

Tyrell who was still watching him but seemed to be losing hope. Awesome, he thought. My inside man... *Don't lose faith in me now.* He made a move toward Tyrell which heightened Tyrell's attention.

Will doubted Tyrell had seen what Will just had. Even if he did, it wouldn't mean anything to him. Will realized, while dodging chairs to get to the counter, he didn't have time to explain any secret rendezvous between two unlikely characters. Will simply had to get into those hallways, so they didn't get too far away.

At the counter, Will hoped his urgent expression would clear his way to Tyrell's back door. If it didn't, Tyrell's massiveness would stop him dead. With his chicken debt looming, a slick explanation might be Will's only option.

He didn't wait to get the go ahead, though. He jumped the counter.

***

That left Tyrell standing there dumbfounded. He had a kid in his store that he needed to do something about, but Danny suddenly passed by handing out donut hole samples in his Pubes wannabe get up. Tyrell waived his head for a second look.

Tyrell was still unsure about Will, and seeing Danny made his head shake. Before moving to flush out Will, he saw Javier watching Danny too. Javier's hands were full, and suddenly, down went the taco shells.

CHAPTER 29

Will peeked his head around the corner then stepped out from Tyrell's kitchen. He quickly stepped back when two security guards whisked by. *Shit.* He looked down at his clothes. He didn't blend in particularly well, and getting caught down here would probably get him banned from the mall for good. *If anyone could kill this awesome roadshow, it would be these guys, and look at who I run into first.*

Will had another problem with being back here that he hadn't thought of until now. He didn't have a clue where these halls led. He was relieved that he eluded the peering eyes of security, but he needed these guys. Who better could show him around? Reluctantly, Will followed them as they disappeared around a corner.

He had no intentions of a grand disturbance or awkward introductions. Sure he was capable of that, but Will was also great at being invisible. These guys weren't about to get any special treatment. He would just let them lead the way. Hopefully, their tour would tell Will everything he needed to know.

"That's as far as you can go," Will heard someone say.

He spun around. He was sure another guard had seen him from behind, but he was alone. He leaned back and breathed a huge sigh of relief. *So, these guys were talking to someone else. But who?* Will pressed on cautiously.

"And this is what we'll use, right?"

That was Chester. Will was sure of it. He slammed himself up against the wall. Now he had three to deal with, and all of them were massively bigger than he was. He looked down the hall, the other way. This was definitely a bad idea. He'd escaped raging rhinos before in these exact halls. Expecting to do it again was simply pressing his luck.

Will couldn't resist the opportunity, though. Good decision or bad, Will was determined for success. He had found Chester without even trying, so luck was on his side. What else could he find out here? The prospect of that was something he could not ignore. He inched closer to the corner.

"In and out."

Leigh this time? Okay, Leigh and Chester teaming up with two security guards. Will gulped with wide eyes at the thought of what might be going on. Even if they ended up dragging him out of here gagged and cuffed, there was no way Will was abandoning this now.

"Just the two of you—"

"At ten. By eleven, we'll be bouncin' off the rafters in this place," Chester said.

Will couldn't believe what he was hearing. How could Leigh go from being so disgusted with Pubes and his sex show, to hooking up with Chester in the basement of the food court? That's what was going on here, right? It had to be what they were planning. What else could it be? He scoured his thoughts to be sure he had all the facts straight. He shook his head in disbelief.

And the luck of Will being down here to witness all of this... He'd just stumbled onto a priceless piece of food court gossip. He remembered Pubes's picture spreading throughout the food court like Leigh's home remedy goo: the stuff he was using on his hair. News like this ranked right up there with that picture. Well, maybe not that hot, but Will thought there must be a way to get this working in his favor.

Will stayed right where he was. He could hear everything, and he couldn't risk blowing it now. He had quick thoughts theorizing the exploitation. He'd let the crew in on it, setting up Chester as a closet romantic. He shook his head. If the *Bitches* knew Chester was secretly interested in someone like Leigh... *Yeah, the Bitches were a better choice.* How about going straight to Chester, and hang it in front of him in return for a prominent position with the crew. He nodded. *That worked. Definitely, that will put me right on the bench with the rest of the crew.*

Then the reality set in. This involved Leigh, and that meant it would be a huge problem for Pubes. But Pubes against Chester over a girl... How would that go down? There was no way around it for Will, though. Despite everything he would be giving up, and what he would be getting Pubes into, Will had to go to Pubes with this.

Will peeped his head around the corner. One security guard was checking a door. The other one was with Chester and Leigh.

"Okay, it's all set." Chester slapped a bill into the guard's hand. He smiled and wrapped his arm around Leigh. "Time to make history, babe." He smiled as though even his teeth had muscles.

Leigh, on the other hand, looked concerned but determined. Will wanted to get her attention, but that would be a mistake. He simply had to get out of here and get this to Pubes.

Will turned back and realized he wasn't sure how to get back to where he came from. He panicked a little. He looked to the others. One of the guards had turned away from them. He headed straight for Will as he pocketed the bill. Will snapped back, flat against the wall. He made a break for what he thought was Tyrell's door.

***

Will burst in.

Tyrell reacted like a street fighter which stopped Will instantly. He closed his eyes expecting a pounding. Great, he thought. First security, then Chester, and now this. Seconds passed, and there was no punch.

Will opened his eyes slowly. He saw Tyrell had noticed who it was and backed off.

The two security guards passed by the open door. Will stayed still, praying they would keep going. They did.

Will asked, "Can you get me back in here, tonight?"

Tyrell was lost for words: not the reaction Will was hoping for. Telling him would guarantee entry, but he didn't know Tyrell well enough. He didn't know if he could trust him which was something Will didn't have time to worry about. He just had to get back in here.

"At Ten. Me and Pubes. Some cover for your cover man," Will said.

Tyrell stepped back, shook his head and threw his arms up. *Come on, man. Don't bail on me now.* The look on Tyrell's face didn't seem to be about backing out, though. He seemed shocked, concerned, even worried, like *I'm not into that kinda shit* worried.

Will clued into Tyrell's homophobic dilemma. "No, man, it's nothin' like that." Will's mind raced for a solution to get Tyrell on board without telling him why. "If I can get him here, he might get back what he needs."

Tyrell was noticeably confused, but he seemed

211

intrigued as well.

"What I need; what *you* need," Will said.

Tyrell hesitated with a head tilt. He was trying to figure Will out, making sure he wasn't being scammed. Will felt like he was going to lose him if he didn't say something. But what could he say that hadn't already been said?

Just tell him, dammit! What harm is it going to do? Will looked back at Tyrell: both as confused as the other. For some reason Will didn't feel like he could say anything. This was for Pubes to find out first. He would tell Pubes, and Pubes would react. It was as simple as that. Anything slipping out could jeopardize that opportunity. If Will was any kind of friend, he owed Pubes that.

But what good would it do Pubes if he couldn't get in here to do something? Tyrell could guarantee access, right where Pubes needed to be, just at the right time. No one else could do that for him. Other than having the information about Leigh and Chester, even Will was useless. Will opened his mouth but hesitated with the words.

Tyrell shook his head as if to clear what he was thinking. "I need to sell chicken. Is this gonna put wings in my fryer?"

Will closed his mouth and forced his lips shut. He smiled then licked them with a satisfactory head tilt. "Fried chicken or fried Pubes. Something's gonna get cooked."

CHAPTER 30

Will used the Beautiful Brilliance kiosk to hide himself. He'd been here for a while, scouting out the food court for more suspicious activity from Chester or Leigh. He hadn't seen either of them again, and nothing seemed out of the ordinary. He may not have had all the facts straight, but something was up between them.

He could have just sat in the food court like he always did, but he wasn't sure how he would react if Leigh saw him there. The kiosk wasn't much good either because she had a tendency to sneak up on him, but at least he wasn't an sitting duck. His only goal in staying here was to get more information. If he was going to Pubes with this, he wanted to be sure about what he would tell him.

He continued to watch the food court, but it was almost empty now. He looked at his cell phone, frustrated. "Shit, Pubes, cut the drama," he said to himself.

He wished, for once, things would go his way. All Pubes had to do was answer. But he didn't, so once again Will faced going to his place. He shook his head knowing it was inevitable. The last thing Will needed right now was to have to knock on that front door, but he couldn't leave Pubes out of this.

He also wasn't sure how Pubes would react. Face-to-face wasn't the best case scenario in Will's opinion. The next move was on him, however. Without him doing something, nothing would be happening for Pubes or him. That, Will was convinced of.

Satisfied that he wasn't going to get any further from hanging out here, he began to walk through the mall while thumbing out another text message.

***

Will checked his watch then hesitated to knock on Pubes's front door. It was late, so he wondered if that would make things worse for him. During the whole ride on his bike over here, he'd tried to talk himself out of doing this, but he never considered the time. Now, at the front door, it was his main concern. The last time he was here it was daytime, and he had Leigh with him. "Did I kiss my mother today?" He looked around, confirming what he already knew. He was alone.

He knocked; no answer. "Shit! They just had to pick

tonight for family night." Really, he was relieved, but no one being here wasn't doing him any good. He quickly thought of *Plan B*, but he didn't have a *Plan B*. His only strategy was to get this dirt to Pubes, ASAP.

He pulled his cell phone from his pocket to check for messages. *None.* He already knew that. He sighed. He knocked again, harder, expecting no response.

Suddenly, an electric saw sang out with its horrific whine. It revved twice then stopped.

Will nearly shit himself, right there, on the spot. He froze. No doubt, that started just for him. He turned for a quick exit. He grabbed the handle bar of his BMX, but the door popped open.

Norma stood there, stone faced.

If he'd been looking away from the house, he could have mounted his bike and bolted from the scene of the crime. But he wasn't looking away. His body pointed toward the street, but his eyes had never left the door. Now he was staring at Norma, and he couldn't let go of her gaze.

"Hi, Will. Would you like to come in?"

Will didn't answer. *Augh, no. Doesn't the look in my eyes; the fear on my face; the piss stain on my pants tell you that?* He touched his crotch just to be sure it was still dry.

When she asked the question, the tone in her voice was completely normal, but she looked like she was from another planet. Will could tell she didn't see his fear, though. If he left, she probably wouldn't even remember him being there. The prospect of him going in seemed bizarre to Will, but what choice did he have?

"Please," she said.

***

The daze in Norma's eyes is what drew Will inside, but now he stood at the entrance in awe while Norma cleared some slippers from the welcome mat in the foyer.

Will couldn't believe what he saw. "It looks—"

Norma's head popped up with renewed energy. "You think so, Will."

Beyond her, the downstairs hallway was immaculate. Hardwood shone; decor was exquisite. The last time Will was here it looked like a firing range for nail gun enthusiasts. Now, this could have been on the cover of Home and Garden.

Miraculously, Will didn't feel all that threatened anymore. The colors were warm and pleasant. New furniture brightened the entrance and what he could see of the family room. He looked at Norma. Her expression pleaded for his acceptance. It was obvious that she was so tired, even Will's praise would be good enough.

"Without Hubert's help to finish up…" Norma looked away, exhausted. She turned to the stairs but didn't dare go there.

Will hadn't seen them when he first entered. They were in plain view, but the beauty before him must have been a distraction. Now, Will understood Norma's look of defeat. The stairs reminded him of where he was: disaster in paradise.

Ralph appeared from upstairs. He was handyman crazed with a circular saw powered up and ready to go. "If I get these headers out tonight, Norma, we'll be cuttin' noses in the mornin'."

***

Hubert lay on his bed staring at the ceiling. He wondered when the power tools would stop. With the final touches done downstairs, he thought his father would call it a day. He should have known better. When Ralph was on a roll, something was going to be ruined, even at this time of night.

Will slid in. He pushed his back against the door as if being seen would be critical. At first they were both silent. Will seemed relieved that he'd made it here, all in one piece.

"We should leave now before the whole place collapses," Will said. He turned the door handle as if he was going to look out but decided against it.

"It's been a long day, Will. I'm gonna crash."

Will pulled on the handle to be sure the door was shut.

"Under the soft sound of spinning metal and splintering wood?"

Hubert turned away.

"How do you go from crazy to crazier? Nice job downstairs by the way," Will said.

Hubert knew Will was right. It had been crazy in here today, and it sounded like things were about to get crazier. Having Will here wasn't making things easier, though.

"They needed my help. Now, what do you need?"

Will hesitated. To Hubert, the question didn't need an answer. He knew what Will was here for. It had always been that way, and nothing was any different now. He really wished Will would leave, so he could just sleep.

"You're right, Pubes. It has been all about me. But you had a good thing going too."

"Had... Good choice of words."

Damn, he's not going anywhere. Hubert certainly knew Will's motive, but he didn't think he would open this conversation with Leigh.

"Yeah. I saw her today." Will waited for a reaction. "With Chester."

Hubert snapped up. "What?"

"That's why I'm here, Pubes. She was with him. First in the food court, then the hallway."

Hubert thought about that for a second. He had never imagined Leigh being interested in Chester. In fact, she'd purposely stayed away from all he had to offer. She'd told him that: *not all girls think alike*. Actually, she had said that to Will...

Hubert flew into Will's face. "You're full of shit!"

Will didn't back down. "They're up to something. Tonight." He checked his watch. "Right now."

Hubert read his face. He backed away. He knew Will well enough. It wasn't often he could take Will seriously, but this time he didn't seem to be kidding around. "So, let her. If that's what she wants."

Hubert turned away. He couldn't care less. At least that was the impression he tried to leave, which couldn't have been further from the truth. He sighed, already giving up his poker face. His acting probably wasn't convincing anyway.

Will grabbed him and spun him around. "Come on, man. You're not gonna sit here and get—"

"And get my life back? Yeah, that's exactly what I'm gonna do."

The circular saw revved. Hubert grimaced while closing his eyes. Will had him by the short and curlies—*by the Pubes*... Hubert shook his head. It couldn't have been at a worse time.

"Well, it looks like the stairs are next," Will said.

Hubert broke away. *Okay, so he says she's with Chester. What exactly am I going to do about that?*

"I'm not asking you to be someone you're not. Not this time," Will said.

Hubert was quiet, and Will just watched him. *Ignoring it is probably not the best option.*

"I just think you should keep what you've got. For guys like us, Pubes, that's like a speck of gold in a pile of sawdust."

The saw started, full time. Hubert couldn't help but think Will had this all timed out with Ralph.

"You can stay here and cut stairs at midnight," Will yelled above the noise.

It stopped.

"Or come with me, and finish what you've started."

CHAPTER 31

Tyrell sat in a van parked in the mall parking lot. He watched one of the security guards manning the door. As far as Tyrell knew, security guards weren't invited to this intimate party. *Security, at this time? That don't make sense.* He nodded slowly. He couldn't help feel that he was being played.

"Kid's messin' with the wrong dude if he's intending to set this motherfucker up," Tyrell said to himself.

He checked his side view mirrors to confirm no one was sneaking up on him. He considered getting out. He couldn't see enough.

His cell phone lit up. He tapped it on the dash without picking it up. "You told me ten, little man. This ass ain't sittin' here all night."

He caught some movement at the side of the building. "Hold it." He focused on what he thought he saw. "There they are, your headline act. This show's ready to roll."

***

Hubert watched Will take his phone away from his ear. Will's story about Leigh and Chester still didn't make any sense, but Will was talking to someone about something. Even though Hubert was skeptical, Will had convinced Tyrell by the sounds of it. Of all people, that certainly couldn't have been an easy task, Hubert thought.

"That's your wake up call. It's now or never, Pubes."

Hubert paced the room. *Will's a drama queen. That's for sure.* That, combined with not wanting to believe Will's story, had Hubert trying to talk himself into just ignoring all the hype Will had created. But deep down Hubert knew he couldn't just sit in his bedroom and do nothing. If it was a hoax, or some messed up scheme Will had dreamed up, what would be the difference? It wouldn't be the first time Hubert had followed Will into craziness. If Hubert continued hanging around with Will, it certainly wouldn't be the last.

"Come on, Pubes. I'll be right there with ya."

"We're talkin' Chester here. He'll clean us both out," Hubert said.

"I can deal with Chester." Will straightened up. He sucked in his gut, but he lost it right away. "Hardwood support, brother. I'm your front line of hardwood support."

A distraction, maybe, but not likely able to do anything that will keep the hound off. Hubert shook away that thought realizing he was actually believing this.

Will stopped Hubert from pacing. "From one loser to another. Let's kick some ass."

Hubert smiled, proud of his friend's tenacity. He shook his head knowing Will would take one in the gut for him. He didn't have to. He didn't even have to be here telling Hubert this. That must mean Will was on to something...

"In your case, get some," Will said.

Hubert suddenly decided he was thinking too much. He bolted for the door. Love him or hate him, Will's eyes were convincing enough for Hubert to follow his lead.

The torn up stairway could have been disastrous, but Hubert took the obstacle in three leaps down. He got through the front door without even noticing his mother or father.

Outside, Hubert noticed Will was right with him. Will mounted his bike. "Jump on!"

Without any time for second guessing, Will had them both rolling down the driveway and into the street. Hubert rode the rear wheel pegs like it was a tandem BMX bike. It was clear sailing, despite the skipping pedal crank.

***

Tyrell was out of his van now, anxious to get on with everything Will had promised. Tyrell wanted to be inside the mall. He had access, but he knew that was what Will needed him for. Tyrell's patience was running out as was Will's time. Despite his promise to wait here, Tyrell was missing out, so Will would soon be left to figure things out for himself.

He reached through the van window and struggled to get his phone from the dash.

***

Hubert could hear Will's phone ringing. Will tried to get it, but that broke his defective peddling rhythm.

The bike swerved, almost dumping both of them. Severe road rash was imminent as Hubert watched the pavement whiz by, too close for comfort. Hubert was able to shift from the back, bringing the bike back in balance.

Hubert took the phone from Will's pocket.

***

Tyrell's eyes were nearly leaving his face. Seconds were being lost, and he couldn't deal with it anymore. "You can't just leave me here, dude. There's nasty things goin' on in there, and I've got chicken to fry," he said into his cell phone.

***

Hubert snapped the phone shut. He screamed at Will. "Faster!"

"What?!? What'd he say?"

"We can't leave him there doin' nasty things with his fried piece of chicken." Hubert thought about what he'd just said. "Or something like that."

"Shit!" Will picked up the pace.

"Move it, Will!"

Hubert shifted back as Will stood up. Hubert realized what was going to happen just as Will hammered the broken crank. It slipped. Will crashed forward: a crotch collision with the handle bar stem.

Will hit the ground and let out an extremely sympathetic groan.

Hubert didn't miss a beat. He launched himself off the crashing bike and ran hard to make up for lost time.

Hubert looked back to see if Will was okay. He was back at it with the bike: one hand on the bars, the other holding his nuts, and one foot doing all the peddling.

Hubert knew Will would relentlessly keep up from behind. Hubert looked forward again. He was relieved that Will was such a trooper, until he saw *the hill...*

***

Hubert sped around a corner and into the mall parking lot. He headed straight for the van. Other than that, the parking lot was empty. He blasted past it toward the only door in sight.

Hubert grabbed the door handle and pulled. The door didn't budge. He looked back to the van. Will was there with his tongue almost touching the ground. For him, the van was far enough.

Will yelled, "Pubes, not there!"

***

Tyrell led the way with Hubert anxiously following. Will was right beside him. They rounded a corner to the loading door they had escaped from before.

Mark was sitting on some of his empty bread boxes. He spotted Tyrell. "Alright, Ty, man. I thought she was all mine, but I'm cool with it," Mark said. He took in most of what was left of his joint.

Hubert rushed for the door. "Don't even fuckin' think about it." He pulled the handle. It was locked. He turned back, quick.

Mark and Tyrell watched him with Will in between.

Will slipped back.

Mark and Tyrell looked at each other, real serious.

Mark broke up. He held up his key card. "You think

I'm gonna leave her open so anyone can slip right in?"

Suddenly, Rand appeared. He rushed to the door and slid his card. "Gotta save Danny from this popularity nightmare."

He was inside in a flash with Hubert right behind.

***

Will stood with Tyrell and Mark watching the door slowly close. Will struggled to figure out Rand's logic. He also couldn't figure out where all the people seemed to be coming from or why they were here at all.

Will understood what Tyrell was doing. He set it up with Tyrell to meet here. But Mark, Rand...

"Holes too. It's gonna be a decent spread," Mark said.

CHAPTER 32

Hubert watched Will drifting slowly through the table section of the food court in a current state of shock. Hubert wasn't far away. He was shocked too but annoyed at the same time.

All around him booze flowed and bodies were grinding. The food court was alive. Techno dance music filled the dark atmosphere, but lights were everywhere.

It was possible Will knew about this all along, and his current state of awe was just an act. Hubert doubted it, though. It was more likely Will had jumped to conclusions at the first sight of seeing Leigh and Chester together.

How this after-hours party came into being didn't matter anyway. What mattered was that everyone who would have been in the locker room would also be here. That included Chester, Virginia, and of course Leigh. He sighed at the thought of having to deal with this.

He looked around to see what he was up against. Never had he seen the food court anything like this. Along with a crowded dance floor in the table section, some of the food vendors were setting up, eager for business.

Hubert saw lights flicker on at Chicken Fried Right. Tyrell worked frantically to get his shop ready for business.

Mark feverishly did the same in the dark at Mark Saint John's Fried Burgers. Mark's store sign flickered. It briefly displayed, *Mark Saint John's Fried Burgers*. Then, *Mark aint Fried* . It flickered again then stayed lit, bright: *Mark Saint John's Fried* .

Mark stood at the counter: a one man team, with stacked burgers and piles of fries, ready for serving.

Hubert saw Will beaming at him from the dance floor. With his arms spread out, Will basked in all the surrounding activity. "Not exactly what I was expecting," he said despite all the surrounding noise.

"From crazy, to crazier, to what now, Will?" Hubert asked the question, but he doubted Will could hear or understand any of it. Judging by the looks of him, Will didn't appear concerned about the same things Hubert was anyway.

Danny cruised by and slipped an advertisement into Hubert's hand. He looked at it. It was a topless picture of Danny holding boxes of *Only Donut Holes*.

Will kept moving in circles with his arms aimlessly

leading the way, right in the middle of all the action. "Christ, Pubes, look around. We made it. I'm here."

"I'm happy for you," Hubert replied without caring if he'd heard. Hubert turned away. He started to leave.

"So you're shippin' without Leigh?"

Hubert stopped. *I guess he did hear.* He turned back surprised to see Will right next to him.

"She might not need your super-human pubic power, but a little seventeen-year-old immaturity might be nice."

"Well, I've got neither, so I'll leave it to you." Hubert stepped away, right into Chester.

"Creepers are usually dealt with by security, but for you I'll make an exception," Chester said.

Chester grabbed him. A crowd started to form. Hubert broke free.

"I was just leaving."

"No, you're not. You put on such a good show last time, I sold tickets for the finale."

Hubert saw Will melting into the surrounding gawkers. He disappeared. *So much for all that distraction, or hardwood support, or whatever he said he'd do that convinced me to come here.*

"So, the penis thing's a wash, at least I hope you washed it."

Chester looked around for some audience reaction. It appeared to Hubert that being on stage seemed to be an issue for Chester. He probably wasn't concerned about Hubert at all. All Chester cared about was saving face with his admirers.

"Looks like you're still having dreams of rising to great heights."

Again, Chester expected something, but this crowd only appeared to be waiting for the imminent beating.

"Don't worry, Chester, I'm no threat to you. You get the panty prize, by default."

Chester chuckled but quickly looked to the crowd. Finally, they laughed. He snapped back and grabbed Hubert by the neck. "Get this straight, Pubes, Hubert, whoever the fuck you are. No one like you *threatens* a dude like me."

Hubert gulped. He fought to get words out. "No one like me cares." He cringed with what might happen after saying that.

"If you had Virginia Almond shaking her dripping fingers in your face shouting do something, you'd care."

Hubert tried to wiggle free, but Chester was clamped on tight.

"And since you already did *something*, guess what, it's my turn."

Chester was primed.

"Give it up, Chester."

Hubert turned to see Virginia step into view.

"You're not funny." She focused on Hubert. "And neither are you."

Because of being held in a near death choke hold,

Hubert actually felt relieved to see Virginia. She had to be Chester's soft spot. Hubert looked around frantically to see what else might get him out of this.

Will was nowhere to be seen. Hubert noticed Danny lurking throughout the crowd handing out cards. Danny was no good to him, and everyone else just watched. Nothing was going in Hubert's favor. It looked like he was completely on his own.

Virginia headed directly for Hubert. Chester let him go.

"You're right. There was nothing funny about it. I'm really sorry," Hubert said.

Her approach continued. "Don't be so quick to show your easy side." She got there and smoothed his shirt where Chester left his mark. "Especially when I've been drinking." She rubbed up against him.

Hubert pushed her away. "Jesus Christ! This is what you're all pumped up for, Will?" He looked for Will, but he wasn't there.

The rest of the party was, though. Hubert looked over them all. "Is this it? These two drive your world?"

Chester and Virginia stood next to each other.

"The only thing they're good for is each other, and they can't even figure that out." He singled out a group of guys watching. "What happened to all the T-Woks hats you guys had? Did Chester decide they had to go?"

Danny was in this group. Hubert saw him because he was a standout, pretty much like Hubert had always been.

Danny realized he was the only one with a hat.

Hubert turned to a group of girls. "And you guys were drooling all over me. Virginia decides who's hot this week, right?"

Hubert pointed to Chester and Virginia. "Why? Why these two?"

He saw Rand standing next to them: another misfit in a crowd of extras. He was fixated on Danny across the floor.

Hubert ran to the edge of the crowd. He grabbed a guy and a girl. "Why not these two?" He pointed to another guy and girl. "Or those two. Why not them?" He shook his head in disbelief. "Why does anyone get so much power?" He addressed everyone. "No one can change who we are. Can't we just figure things out for ourselves?"

"Only if you have enough strength to believe in yourself."

Those words came from somewhere in the crowd, but Hubert knew the voice; he knew who it was. Leigh appeared with Will beside her.

Hubert couldn't help but notice Rand and Danny locked up in each other.

Leigh continued, "What about you, Pubes? Do you believe in Hubert?"

Hubert thought about it. He did believe in himself. He just had trouble with everyone else telling him he shouldn't.

"I don't think belief is enough, though," Leigh continued. "Love is the only thing that can make you rise above." She looked deep into his eyes. "So, what about you? Do you believe in love, Hubert?"

Hubert returned her stare. At that moment, it was only him and her in the whole food court. Nothing else mattered. For Hubert, whatever he did next would mean everything. Chester and Virginia wouldn't be able to change anything. Will couldn't rescue him. He closed his eyes.

"You know, if I turn away right now, I'd be walking away from just that, love." Hubert started to leave but stopped.

He saw Rand turn away from Danny.

"But, if I look love straight in the eye..." Hubert turned to Leigh. "I face what I fear the most." He looked away to break the tension. "Don't get me wrong. I'm not afraid of being with you. I'm just afraid of what's expected." He looked back. His eyes were pleading. "I'm just not ready for that."

Hubert rushed close to Chester and Virginia.

"Maybe they are." He moved quickly toward Will.

"Will is, at least he says he is." He pointed to everyone around. "Maybe they all are, or maybe..." He stopped. "Just maybe, they're not."

He turned back to Leigh. "I'm not. I know I'm not. But Will did the right thing; you did the right thing. You moved me past hiding from it."

He broke away. "So now if I walk away—"

"You'll believe in Hubert?"

Hubert smiled. He tucked in his shirt, pulled up his pants. He tightened his belt. "Well, one thing's for sure. I've always believed in love."

He smiled. "Love what you do. That's me... Hubert."

Rand and Danny busted out from the crowd and crashed into a flamboyant embrace.

The tension broke. Music and grinding started again. Even a little plain old dancing.

Leigh stepped toward Hubert. He did the same. They met among everyone else.

She reached out for both of his hands. They touched. Meaningful smiles came from both of them.

Leigh slowly grabbed his shirt at the waist. She pulled it out of his pants. "That's going too far."

She took his hand, and they walked away.

***

Will danced with Elle and Jane. Hubert and Leigh passed by him.

"Remember that Will guy he was talking about? That's me."

The girls just nodded to the beat.

"Ready and..." He cleared his throat; he flipped his

eyebrows. "Willing."

CHAPTER 33

Even though Chester had always pretty much controlled the work he and the crew did in the food court, there were times when his job actually required effort. This was one of those moments. He tried to convince himself that a little hard work wouldn't do him any harm, but his habit of doing next to nothing had an overruling effect.

He cringed as he moved a table away from the seating area. He looked up to see the rest of the crew struggling too. Floors were being washed; they scrubbed tables to remove the grime left from their neglect.

Chester saw Rod supervising with an iron fist. Rod had found out about the party, and since then, it was like the crew was being sentenced to food court community service. Chester didn't know if Rod was actually taking his job seriously, or if he was pissed that he hadn't been invited.

Rod's eyes narrowed in on Chester, probably because Chester was doing nothing again. Chester continued with the tables when he noticed the food stores start opening.

***

Will stood alone which was certainly nothing unusual for him. This time, however, it felt right. There was nothing awkward about him being there. Others beside him, in front and behind him, were there for the same reason. For the first time really, he felt like he fit in with this crowd.

He knew why. It had nothing to do with image or being like everyone else. It was all because of Pubes being Hubert. But for Will, Pubes would never be the Hubert everyone here had completely accepted. For Will, that Hubert would always be Pubes. He smiled thinking about the nickname he'd created. If he had done nothing else for his best friend, he'd given him a name that would never be forgotten.

He looked around at spotless floors. Cheap, last minute floral arrangements decorated the tables. All the shops were fully staffed and busy, literally cooking for a feast.

He saw the table section overflowing with others his age. It was like a different place completely, but it was still the same food court. Change had come, though. The food court shone like the military had taken over.

"And by the powers invested in me…"

Will joined everyone as they abandoned their seats. They rushed forward like they were about to get the final song at a rock concert.

"I now pronounce you—"

Off queue, The Wedding Song started.

Applause burst out.

The crowd in front of Will separated to expose Rand and Danny standing at a makeshift altar in front of the Only Donut Holes store front.

Will saw Hubert standing beside Danny; Leigh was beside Rand.

The Minister gave his nod of approval.

Rand and Danny kissed. Long, passionate: sickening really.

The congregation broke into celebration. It quickly became an underage techno bar in the food court.

***

Will took a mic from the head table. He mouthed something, but music drowned him out.

He tapped the mic. He tried again: nothing.

He looked at a speaker beside him. He moved in front of it with the mic behind his back. Nothing happened. He turned to the speaker and looked at the mic. He dropped it.

The thud startled him. Then came the screech.

He scrambled for the mic and made a quick recovery.

"Excuse me." He reached into his pocket and pulled out a skin care sample. He considered keeping it, but too many people were watching. He tossed it then tried again.

He pulled out a piece of paper. "Could Chester come up here?" He waited, but Chester didn't show. "Has anyone seen Chester?" He looked throughout the crowd: no Chester. "Someone told me to open with a joke, but I guess I can't."

Some laughed. Not many, though.

Tony stepped out from the crowd. "Chester's not funny."

That got the reaction Will was looking for. He soaked up the attention, until he saw Chester sitting alone with Virginia.

Their eyes locked. Will panicked a little. He resorted to his paper. "The fine folks who make the food in this place would like to present their offering to the..." He looked at Rand and Danny. "To this extremely strange, but somehow inspirational, couple."

He saw Pubes and Leigh standing beside Rand and Danny. They smiled back at him.

"So stand back and let the food parade proceed."

Behind the tables, in front of each store, there was a lavish display of their particular offering.

"When they're done, the rest is yours."

Shirley from *Salads Like Mom Makes* was first. She proudly walked toward the head table with lush salads.

Abid carried a tray of subs from *Sub Attack* next, followed by Rocco proudly holding *Italy's Best* fast food cuisine.

Mark was next sportin' *Mark Saint John's Fried Burgers* with Tyrell following and his abundant selection of *Chicken Fried Right*.

Tung hit the floor along with his screaming chefs, each carrying a dish and wearing a *T-Woks* hat.

Bringing up the tail end was Javier carrying a huge tray of elaborately stuffed *Mexican Heaven* tacos.

Will watched them make their way to the head table.

The tingling of glasses started.

Rand and Danny prepped up for another guy-on-guy performance. The crowd shouted their disapproval.

Rand and Danny glared back with resentment. They walked away arm-in-arm, content with each other.

The tingling continued, louder.

Will knew what the crowd demanded. Left there standing were Hubert and Leigh. They looked at each other, then the crowd. Yep, it was confirmed. This tingle was for them.

They looked back at each other. Leigh reached for his hand.

The food was being dropped off in front of them.

They got closer.

The tingling…

Finally, they kissed. Soft, gentle: just like a first kiss should be.

Will watched Javier still approaching with his tray. He began to tear up. The tray started to wobble.

The crowd reacted. He stumbled for a recovery. The tray stabilized.

With it under control, Javier smiled.

Everyone cheered.

Javier took a confident step right in front of the head table.

Oh no, the sample. Will saw it before Javier even had a chance. In fact, Javier was too busy basking in the limelight to notice anything else.

The tray went airborne. One taco broke away from all the others.

***

Hubert didn't see anything coming, but he shuffled knowing something was up.

He turned, shocked by the incoming taco that landed straight into his opened mouth.

He chomped down hard and smiled huge, with a mouthful of lettuce.

###

ABOUT THE AUTHOR

A truly great thing about writing is being able to express our inner thoughts for others to enjoy—or enjoy to hate, evident in the no holds barred review process we writers quickly become subject to. We call this Freedom of Speech or Freedom of Expression: an international human right in all democratic societies.

However, even though we can write what we want, we will always have a cloud over our creative heads. This gloom comes in the form of censorship, ratings, political correctness, race, sexual preference; and the list continues... Sure, if you're writing just for yourself, you probably don't have to worry about these things. But writers who are trying to create an audience have to consider all of this when exercising their right.

Economics plays a big part in a writer's freedom too. Any publisher will encourage their writers to brand themselves. This is why we see authors writing in a specific genre; they write a series to give their audience more about the hero they've created. Although this is certainly a good strategy for building a writing career, it creates another roadblock which prevents us from telling you what we really feel.

It doesn't have to be this way, though. There's a phrase in the writing world: *Concept is King.* Not genre; not franchise heroes, but it's the story idea that captures an audience above all else. The subject is up for debate, but any writer will tell you the same thing. When you come up with a *Jurassic Park,* the world stops, and the story must be written.

This happened to me with *Circumcised at Seventeen.* Before this story I had two novels completed: *Purified*—a medical thriller, and *Sins of a Priest*—a supernatural thriller. *Circumcised at Seventeen* took me pretty far away from that thriller brand. This story's genre is young adult comedy. At this point I can see any publishers reading this actually cringe… But it's a story that is described in three words; it's extremely unique, and we'll see if it attracts a large audience.

Next up, I'll be heading back into the thriller genre with a sci-fi thriller: *A World Without Roads.* Beyond that I have other comedy ideas and a sport drama concept that I'd like to get into print.

High concepts tend to rule my writing. They're what I search for when I work on new story ideas; they are what motivates me to dive into a new project from scratch. Above all of that, exploring them allows me to express that freedom to write what I want.

If concept truly rules, I may be on to a different approach with branding myself as a concept writer. This thinking among the vast community of writers could generate a fantastic pool of unique stories for readers to enjoy. If publishers are correct with their branding strategies, however, I may be just writing for myself.